"I'm going with you, Josh."

"You're going to stay in the room with the door locked. I don't want you anywhere near this situation."

"You just said it wasn't going to be dangerous," Gina insisted.

"I didn't say that." He cupped her face with one hand. "Let me face the danger. You've faced enough—all your life."

She blinked her eyes to dispel the tears gathering there. Nobody, not her mother, not Ricky, not the DEA, CIA or the FBI, had ever once acknowledged the fear and danger she'd lived with her whole life.

She thought it had come to an end that day at her father's compound, but she couldn't have been more wrong. Only now she had Josh Elliott to protect her, and if he thought she needed to stay in the room for this encounter, she'd do it.

She nodded and sniffed. "All right. I'll wait in the room, but you'd better be careful."

"This is what I do."

Was it? Then what had he been doing at her father's compound the day the men in her life had been killed?

BULLSEYE: SEAL

CAROL ERICSON

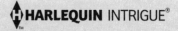
HARLEQUIN INTRIGUE®

To Jeff B., my favorite marine and consultant

Recycling programs for this product may not exist in your area.

ISBN-13: 978-0-373-75699-5

Bullseye: SEAL

Copyright © 2017 by Carol Ericson

Printed in U.S.A.

HARLEQUIN®
www.Harlequin.com

Carol Ericson is a bestselling, award-winning author of more than forty books. She has an eerie fascination for true-crime stories, a love of film noir and a weakness for reality TV, all of which fuel her imagination to create her own tales of murder, mayhem and mystery. To find out more about Carol and her current projects, please visit her website at www.carolericson.com, "where romance flirts with danger."

Books by Carol Ericson

Harlequin Intrigue

Red, White and Built

Locked, Loaded and SEALed
Alpha Bravo SEAL
Bullseye: SEAL

Target: Timberline

Single Father Sheriff
Sudden Second Chance
Army Ranger Redemption
In the Arms of the Enemy

Brothers in Arms: Retribution

Under Fire
The Pregnancy Plot
Navy SEAL Spy
Secret Agent Santa

Harlequin Intrigue Noir

Toxic

Visit the Author Profile page at Harlequin.com.

CAST OF CHARACTERS

Gina De Santos—Her life in a shambles after her drug-dealer father and husband are killed, Gina is trying to get back on track with her son in Miami, but her past threatens their safety until a mysterious navy SEAL appears to protect her.

Josh Elliott—This navy SEAL sniper is responsible for the death of Gina's husband. Since he protected her once, he vows to protect her again—if she'll let him.

Hector De Santos—Gina's father, a drug kingpin, made a fatal mistake getting into bed with a terrorist cell, and that mistake continues to haunt his daughter and grandson.

Ricky Rojas—Gina's dead husband kept secrets and courted her for all the wrong reasons, which may have destroyed her trust in every other man she meets.

RJ De Santos—Gina's son is too young to know his father's and grandfather's business, but not too young to be used as a pawn.

Roger and Tara—These newlyweds on their honeymoon seem to be more interested in Gina and Josh than each other.

Joanna De Santos—Gina's mother has no trouble spending drug money to maintain her lifestyle, until it threatens the family she loves.

Rita Perez—The mother of one of RJ's friends, she's more than happy to have RJ at her home, but can she be trusted?

Vlad—A sniper for the insurgents in the Middle East caused trouble for Josh's sniper team, but this wartime clash has turned into a personal vendetta.

Ariel—The mysterious person on the other end of an email address giving orders to Josh on his mission cares more about bringing down Vlad than protecting Gina.

Prologue

The boy tottered close to the edge of the shimmering pool, and Josh Elliott held his breath. A woman, her long, dark hair falling over one shoulder, swooped in and plucked up the toddler, lifting him over her head. The boy's face broke into a smile, his little body wriggling with joy in his mother's grasp.

Safe in his mother's arms—or he would be once she got the hell out of there.

Josh puffed out of the side of his mouth to dislodge a bug crawling on his face. He'd become part of the dense foliage on the hillside in this southeast corner of Colombia, not far from the Amazon. If this mission took any longer, the plants would grow right over and through him.

The woman dipped next to a chaise longue to grab a towel and tucked it around her child's body. She gave a curt nod to the men gathered at the other end of the pool, and then headed for the house via the sliding glass doors. Josh released a long breath.

A voice crackled in his ear seconds later. "Go time, boys."

Josh swept his M91 away from the retreating figure of the mother and her child and zeroed in on his intended target—her husband.

Ricky Rojas folded his arms, his expensive jacket tightening across his shoulders, as he cocked his head in the direction of the three men seated at the table. What Josh wouldn't give to hear their conversation right now—their plots, their plans—but his SEAL team's assignment didn't include capture and interrogation.

It only included death.

These men had already killed and would kill again. In the crack of two seconds, his team would be responsible for bringing down a high-ranking member of a vicious terrorist cell and the mastermind of a brutal drug cartel…and a few of his associates.

And the father of that child.

Josh swallowed. The kid would get over it, especially after he learned what a scumbag his old man had been. The wife? That might be another story.

A muscle ticked in Josh's jaw. They'd been told to keep the woman out of the range of fire. More senior people than he had made the determination that Gina Rojas had nothing to do with the Los Santos drug cartel.

If they believed the daughter of Hector De Santos, the kingpin of Los Santos, and the wife of Ricky Rojas was an innocent bystander while her father and husband traded arms and passage to the United States for terrorists in exchange for drugs, who was he to question their common sense?

A pretty face could still buy wiggle room out of anything—and Gina Rojas had a pretty face and a body that could bring a grown man to his knees.

Once the kills were accomplished, the CIA would be descending on the De Santos compound to search for leads and evidence, but he and his teammates would be long gone, swallowed up into the Amazon.

A maid scurried from the palatial house to deliver a tray of drinks to the men on the patio. When she disappeared inside, the crackling in his ear resumed.

"All clear. And five, four, three, two…"

At the conclusion of the countdown, Josh dropped his target, and all the other men fell with him courtesy of the other navy SEAL snipers positioned in trees and dug into the hillsides ringing the compound.

The maid rushed from the house and threw

her hands in the air. She must've been screaming because several other servants joined her
on the patio.

Josh shifted his scope to encompass Gina
Rojas emerging from the house, without her
son, thank God. While the domestic staff flailed
and scurried about or dashed off for parts unknown, Gina stood still like a statue amid a bat-
tering sea. She put her arm around the hysterical
maid and surveyed the carnage, her head held
high, her gaze sweeping the hillside.

"Josh. Josh, you on the move?"

"Copy that."

He lowered his sniper rifle from the intrigu-
ing sight of Gina Rojas's unflinching demeanor
and began to break down his weapon.

Either this hit was no surprise to Gina...or
she didn't give a damn.

Chapter One

Thirteen months later.

RJ raised a chubby hand before spinning around and grabbing his new friend by the arm to drag him to the slide.

Gina sniffed as she waved to her son's back.

"It's better than having him cling to your leg, isn't it?" Denise Reynolds, the owner of Sunny Days Daycare, winked.

Gina rubbed the back of her hand across her nose. "Much better, but did he have to get over that stage so quickly?"

"RJ's an outgoing boy. He makes friends quickly, very adaptable."

"He's had to be." Gina hoisted her purse onto her shoulder and shrugged. "There's been a lot of upheaval in his young life."

"I saw from your application that you're relatively new to Miami." Denise bit her lip. "And

I'm sorry about his father, your husband. That he's deceased, I mean."

"Yes, just over a year ago." Gina sniffed again for good measure. "We're still…adjusting."

"Well, I think Sunny Days is just the place for him to adjust. One month and he already has a best friend, who started just a few days after he did."

"He already talks about Diego nonstop. His mother introduced herself to me right away. The boys already had one playdate and we'll be arranging another for them in the next few days." Gina's cell phone buzzed in her pocket, and her heart skipped a beat.

"Everything okay?" Denise tilted her head to one side, her perky blond ponytail swinging behind her.

"Just a pesky client." Gina patted the pocket of her light jacket. "Thanks for everything, Denise."

Gina whipped out her phone as she walked back to her car. She couldn't go into cardiac arrest every time someone sent her a text. Wedging her hip against the cinder block barrier between the daycare's parking lot and the walkway to the center, she swiped her fingertip across her phone's display.

Then her heart skipped two beats as she read

the familiar words. Where are the drugs? Where are the weapons, *paloma*?

The same two questions, along with the endearment, texted to her every day for almost a week now, from the same unknown number. She'd responded to the text in several different ways already.

Wrong number.

Wrong person.

I'm calling the police.

It didn't seem to matter what she texted back. The same two questions came back at her each day as if on autopilot—with the same endearment. Only Ricky had called her *paloma*... when things were good, but that was impossible. Wasn't it?

She *could* call the police. She snorted and dropped her cell phone in her pocket as she opened her car door. Then she'd have to go through the whole process of explaining who she was and watch the officers' faces change from expressions of concern to scowls of suspicion. They might even call in her old pals at the Drug Enforcement Administration, and they could start grilling her again.

She'd take a pass. In the meantime, she'd continue to ignore the texts. The person texting her wouldn't try to make contact…would he? And that person couldn't be Ricky. Ricky was dead…wasn't he?

Glancing over her shoulder, she pulled out of the daycare's parking lot and checked her rearview mirror as she joined the stream of traffic. She had nothing to tell anyone who made contact with her, at least not about any drugs or weapons.

On her way to the realty office, she turned up the music to drown out her own thoughts and the memories of that day at her father's compound in Colombia. The CIA agents who'd swarmed the place after the carnage had interrogated everyone on the property, including her, for several hours.

They'd tossed the place, looking for money, drugs, arms—and they didn't find one single thing. As far as she knew, not even her father's computers had revealed any information about his thriving drug business.

The US and Colombian governments had seized all her father's assets—but they hadn't found everything. Then the CIA turned her over to the DEA and the fun started all over again. She had no desire to repeat that experience.

She wheeled into the parking lot of the realty

office and dragged her bag from the passenger seat as she exited the car. She'd just passed her licensing exam but didn't have any listings of her own yet. She had to start from the bottom and work her way up, but she'd never been afraid of hard work.

The real estate business may not be her calling, but she'd had to find some gainful employment after she'd lost her business—the restaurant-bar she'd developed and run with Ricky before…before.

She slammed the car door. She'd tried bartending since that's what she knew, but that hadn't been her calling either, not if she couldn't run the place, and she didn't like leaving RJ with her mother so many nights of the week.

Gina yanked open the door of the office and waved to Lori, who was on the phone. Lori wiggled her fingers in the air in response.

A stack of binders piled on her desk greeted Gina and she plopped down in front of them with a sigh. Faith, the Realtor she was shadowing, had left a yellow sticky note on the binder at the top of the pile asking her to remove the old listings.

Gina flipped open the binder and perused each page, checking the house against a roster for those listings no longer on the market. For each lucky house that had sold, she slid the flyer from beneath the plastic sheath, making a neat pile on the corner of the desk.

Lori ended her call and slumped in her chair. "Clients from hell right there, but they're looking high-end, art deco in South Beach, and I'm going to do my best to find the perfect place for them. Can you do me a favor?"

"If it involves white binders, I'll pass." Gina heaved the first completed binder off the desk and dropped it to the floor.

"It involves meeting a client at a town house. It's empty. Owners already moved out, and it's an easy show. I'll cut you in on a portion of the commission if this person buys it."

"Is this buyer one of your clients?"

"No. The sellers are my clients. This person is a walk-in. Just called this morning." Lori jiggled a set of keys over her desk. "Easy show."

Gina wrinkled her nose at the rest of the binders. "Sure. Give me the details."

Fifteen minutes later, Gina was sitting behind the wheel of her car with a file folder on the seat beside her, cruising to South Beach. She enjoyed this aspect of the job more than sitting at a desk reviewing Florida property laws and regulations.

As she flew past the strip malls and heavily residential areas, she could understand why Lori wanted to spend her time selling in South Beach instead of this area, but Gina found the relative serenity of the southern end of Dade County preferable to the hubbub in South Beach where she and RJ had landed with Mom after the debacle in Colombia.

Debacle—was that what you called the deaths of your father and husband at the hands of some unknown snipers?

The Spanish-style building came into view on her right, the beige stucco, arched entrances and red-tiled roof a copy of several other residences on the street. This was a town house, not a condo, so it had a door open to the outside and two palm trees graced either side of the entrance.

Her heels clicked on the tiled walkway to the front door, and a palm frond tickled her cheek as she inserted the key into the lockbox. Pushing the door open, she left it wide, surveying the small foyer before taking a small step down to the living room.

She glanced at the flyers in her hand and left a stack on the kitchen counter. She should probably familiarize herself with the place before the potential buyer showed up, starting with the kitchen.

All the appliances cooperated as she flipped switches and turned handles. The kitchen didn't boast the most high-tech gadgetry she'd ever seen, but everything worked and had a neat functionality. She could get used to a place like this.

She had to get out of Mom's condo—and all it represented.

She poked her head into the laundry room off the kitchen, noting the side door to a small patio, and then backtracked to the living room. The gas fireplace checked out, as did the blinds shuttering the arched front window. The sun filtered into the room, as she pulled them back. A set of sliding glass doors to the right led to a small patio, a stucco wall enclosing it.

Finishing up with the half bathroom, she headed up the staircase to investigate the two bedrooms and two bathrooms. The master had a nice walk-in closet, and she mentally filled the racks with her shoes and layered the baskets with her sweaters.

She closed the closet door behind her with a firm click. She was here for the buyer, not herself, even if that buyer *was* late.

She glided into the second room, trying not to imagine RJ's toys stacked in colorful bins against the wall.

A sound from downstairs had her pausing at the window that looked out onto a small patio in the back. She cocked her head, and then heard the shuffling noise again.

She walked to the bedroom door and called out, "Hello? I'm upstairs. I'll be right down. Take a flyer."

Facing herself in the mirrored closet door, she straightened her jacket and smoothed her hands over her dark pencil skirt. For good measure, she rolled open the closet door and peered at the empty rods and shelves. The place looked mint.

As she slid the door back into place, a bang had her jerking and literally clutching the pearls at her neck. What was the buyer doing down there?

She raised her eyes to her reflection and swallowed as the hair on the back of her neck quivered. Why hadn't the client answered her?

She'd taken a safety class as part of getting her Realtor's license and knew the dangers of women flying solo while showing open houses. But this was no open house. Lori had made an appointment with this person, had gotten identifying information from him over the phone.

Sweeping her tongue across her lips, she backed away from the mirror. She strode to the bedroom door, calling out, "Hello? Are you still here?"

She jogged down the stairs, her muscles tense, her senses on high alert. When she reached the bottom step, she tripped to a stop.

The blinds across the window that she'd just

opened now shuttered out the sunlight. Her gaze darted to the front door, now closed.

A clicking noise from the laundry room acted like a cattle prod and she lunged for the purse she'd foolishly left on the kitchen counter. Strapping the purse across her body, she ripped open the side pocket and grabbed her .22, the cool metal of the gun in her hand giving her courage.

She flicked off the safety and rounded the corner of the counter into the kitchen, holding her weapon in front of her. Not a great start to her career as a Realtor, but she'd do what had to be done to protect herself. That much she'd learned from Hector De Santos.

The door from the laundry room to the back of the building stood ajar and Gina crept toward it, locked and loaded.

Her heart pounded as the laundry room door suddenly swung open and a large man filled the frame of the doorway.

She raised her gun and took aim at his head. "Who the hell are you and what are you doing here?"

Chapter Two

Josh didn't trust Gina Rojas as far as he could toss her, but even *he* didn't expect her to hold him at gunpoint this early in their relationship.

"Whoa, there." He raised his hands, his own weapon heavy in the pocket of his jacket. "I'm just here to look at the town house."

She narrowed her dark eyes, her nostrils flaring as if sniffing out his lie. "Why are you sneaking around?"

"Sneaking?" He spread his hands in front of him. "Just thought I'd check out the laundry room and this back door."

"And the blinds?" She didn't seem to be buying any of this since her deadly little .22 was still pointing at his face.

Blinds? "Yeah, the blinds."

"Why'd you close them?"

His pulse ticked up even higher and it had nothing to do with Gina's weapon leveled at him. Someone *had* been here before he'd arrived, had closed the blinds and the front door—and then escaped out the back when he showed up.

"Testing them out." He cleared his throat. "Look, I'm sorry I gave you a scare. I'm really just here to look at the town house if you want to show it to me."

"What's your name?"

Wasn't her arm getting tired hoisting that gun?

She would be expecting the name of the person who'd made the appointment to see the place—and he couldn't give her that.

"I'm Josh Edwards. Is this an open house? I've been looking in this area for a while, saw the for-sale sign, saw the car in the driveway and the open door. I figured I could take a peek." He lifted his shoulders and twisted his lips into what he hoped was a passable grin. "I guess that wasn't such a good idea."

Gina's grip on her gun relaxed. "I'm expecting someone else at any minute."

"Understood. Can you show me around until they get here…without pointing the gun at me?"

Gina lowered her weapon and it dangled at her side, but she shook her cell phone at him in its place. "That other buyer is going to be here soon, and my office knows where I am and when to expect me."

"Good." He dropped his hands. "You can never be too careful."

Especially if you were involved with drug dealers and terrorists. Was that why Gina was so jumpy? And was this buyer she was expecting the one who closed the blinds and hightailed it out the back door when he heard him at the front door? Why would anyone do that, unless the intruder planned to steal Gina's purse, which she'd left out on the counter?

Or unless that buyer had a different motive altogether.

"Let's start over." He edged away from the laundry room and into the kitchen just in case she changed her mind and decided to take a shot at him. About a foot away from her, he extended his hand. "Josh Edwards, and I'm interested in the town house."

She tucked her gun into the purse hanging sideways across her body and took his hand. "Gina De Santos, Four Points Realty, and I'll be happy to show it to you."

De Santos? She'd ditched Ricky's name already?

She strode ahead of him into the living room. "Let's open up those blinds again and get some light in here, since it really is a good feature of the place."

While she tugged on the cords of the blinds, his gaze lingered on her backside, round and full beneath her slim skirt. She hadn't lost anything in the looks department in the past year.

He turned toward the sliding door to the patio. "This is nice. Should get lots of sun."

She joined him, smelling like some tropical hothouse flower. "Yes, but there's enough room out here for a table, a few chairs and an umbrella in case the sun gets too hot. The wall is tall enough to restrict a small dog…or children. Do you and your wife have children?"

"Me? No."

She raised her dark, sculpted brows at him.

Had he come off too strong? He'd decided long ago never to bring kids into this world. Look at her own son.

They returned to the kitchen where she pointed out a few features that held no interest for him at all.

"The laundry room—" she jerked a thumb over her shoulder "—you've already explored. Do you want to go out that back door, or did you see enough?"

He hadn't seen enough. He hadn't seen the person who'd been in the house closing the blinds.

"I'm good."

"You'll love the upstairs. For a single guy like you? Roomy master suite with a second room for an office or gym." Her gaze traveled up and down his body as she brushed past him.

The look she gave him made him hard in all the right places but he'd better rein in his galloping lust or she might pull that gun out on him again. Why'd she think he was a single guy? He'd said no to the kids, but he hadn't denied the wife. Probably had something to do with the look in his own eyes when she waltzed past him.

He followed her up the stairs, pinning his gaze to her swaying hair instead of her swaying derriere. If he could remember that she was most likely complicit in her father's deeds that would be enough to splash cold water on him. How could she not have known what was going on in that compound?

"Here's the master." She stepped aside and gestured him into the room.

He wandered around and poked his head in the closet, which he couldn't imagine filling in a million years. "Impressive."

While she was still talking about east-facing windows and views, he blew past her into the next room, anxious to make his initial report, anxious to get away from Gina De Santos and the way she stirred his blood.

"This room is smaller, has the mirrored closet

doors. Could work as a gym." Again, that appraising inventory of his body that made him want to flex every muscle he had. "Or an office. What is it you do?"

"Software development. I work at home."

"This would be perfect for you."

They completed the tour of the town house and returned to the kitchen where she shoved a flyer at him. "What do you think?"

"I like...everything about it." He tore his gaze away from her liquid brown eyes and squinted at the flyer. "Might be out of my price range, though. Do you have a card?"

"Of course." She flattened her purse against her body as she unzipped the top, and he could see the outline of her gun in the outside pocket.

That purse was specifically designed for a weapon. The lady was serious about her self-defense. But why?

"Here you go." She snapped a gold-embossed card on top of the flyer. "Office number and cell."

He skimmed a finger across the glossy flyer. "This isn't your listing? It says Lori Villanueva is the listing agent."

"I'm helping her out. She was busy today."

Did that mean the intruder hadn't expected Gina to be here? Maybe it was just a thief looking for a quick prize, but then he'd missed the purse on the counter.

"Your original client never showed up."

She gave a little jerk to her shoulders. "Happens all the time."

"Then I'm glad I stopped by, so you didn't have to waste your time."

"I am, too, and I apologize for drawing down on you."

"Perfectly understandable and advisable...for a woman in your position."

She lifted her chin. "My position?"

"A Realtor working on your own. Can't be too careful these days."

"My feelings exactly." She scooped up the rest of the flyers and tapped their edges on the granite. "Call me...if you're interested in the town house."

"Will do." He left her to lock up the place and slid into the front seat of his rental.

He was interested all right—just not in the town house.

Josh pulled out his phone and texted a message to Ariel, his contact person on this assignment. He knew better than to question why he was reporting to a nameless, faceless woman instead of his superiors in the navy.

He'd been pulled off a deployment in Afghanistan and sent to Colombia with a short stop in the United States. His commander had briefed him there and the assignment dictated he return to the United States and make contact with Gina Rojas—De Santos. Done.

Ariel's response instructed him to compile a report on his first meeting…and to pursue the relationship to find out what Ricky Rojas's widow knew.

Easier said than done. He didn't have the savvy of that smooth SOB Slade Gallagher or the aw-shucks cowboy twang of his other teammate Austin Foley.

But he'd definitely seen a spark of interest in Gina's dark eyes when she'd assessed him. He'd had to capitalize on that, since he wasn't ready to tell her he'd been the navy SEAL sniper who'd killed her husband, even if he had been sent to Miami to protect her.

He looked up as Gina exited the town house and swiveled her head in his direction.

Lifting a hand, he pulled away from the curb. He didn't want her to think he was waiting for her or stalking her. She was jumpy enough. He'd have to put that in his report, too.

He made his way back to his hotel in the much more crowded area of South Beach. Whichever government agency was sponsoring this little reconnaissance mission had some deep pockets. Or maybe they'd just put him up in this swanky hotel because of its proximity to Gina's mother's place, who must still be living high on the hog courtesy of her former husband's drug money—not that the DEA could prove it or find it.

Back in his hotel room, Josh flipped open his laptop and wrote up a report on his initial meeting with Gina De Santos. He left out the part about the sparks that had flown between them, although Ariel would probably tell him to use that to his advantage.

He hit Send on the email with its attachment and pushed away from the desk. He wandered to the window with its view of several pastel art deco buildings. At least that's something he'd gotten out of his previous relationship—a little culture thrown in with all the cheating.

Snorting, he turned his back on the art deco and flipped on the TV. He'd already figured out the hotel carried the channel with the UFC fight. He'd take the UFC over art deco any day—maybe that's why his ex cheated on him.

He reclined on the bed, placing his laptop beside him. Wouldn't want to miss an urgent message from Ariel.

He had no idea why the navy was sending a navy SEAL stateside to keep tabs on a dead drug dealer's daughter, but he'd figured it was the same reason why they'd sent two of his sniper unit team members on similar assignments in the past few months—Vlad.

Had their old nemesis really been the man behind the drugs-for-arms deal involving De Santos's cartel, Los Santos?

If that were the case, Josh would be only too happy to thwart Vlad's plans.

The fight proved to be too one-sided to hold his interest, and he clicked through the remote to find something else. As he settled back against the stack of pillows to watch an old comedy, his laptop dinged, indicating a new message.

He dragged the computer onto his lap and double-clicked the email.

Ariel's message left nothing unclear. *Get close to the subject to exploit or protect.*

It didn't sound like Ariel and her bunch, whoever that was, believed Gina was as innocent as the CIA agents did a year ago. Exploit? If Gina had intel about her father's old operation, he'd be expected to get that from her. Protect? If she did have that intel she could be in danger from her father's old associates…or others.

Did Gina think she could play with fire and not get burned?

He dipped his hand in his front pocket and flicked the corner of the card he'd pulled out. Gina's office number and her cell number. Maybe he could offer to buy her a drink for showing him the town house…or demand she buy him one for pulling a gun on him.

Get close to the subject? He had no problem with that order—no problem at all.

GINA PEEKED INTO RJ's room one last time. The soft breathing and tousled, dark hair on the pillow drew her in like a magnet and she tiptoed across the carpet and crouched beside his bed.

She kissed her fingertips and then pressed them against his temple, whispering, "Sleep tight, baby boy."

"He won't even know you're gone. You know what a heavy sleeper he is."

"Shh." Gina sprang to her feet and shooed her mother from the doorway of RJ's room. "Even a heavy sleeper is going to wake up with all your yammering."

Mom placed one hand on her curvy hip and shook her other finger in Gina's face. "You're nervous, aren't you? You haven't been on a date since Ricky's death, and you're scared. Do you want a few tips?"

"From you?" Gina raised her eyebrows. "No, thanks."

"The first tip—" her mother breezed past her and picked up her oversize wineglass "—you should have your date pick you up at home, like a gentleman."

"Meeting him at the bar was my idea. I barely know the guy. I don't want him to know where I live." Gina leaned toward the large gilt-edged mirror above the fireplace and drew her pinky finger along the edge of her lower lip to fix her smudged lipstick.

Mom clicked her tongue. "You have to open up and trust a little, or you'll never get anywhere."

"Like I trusted Ricky?"

"Ricky was such a handsome boy, so charming although a little weak around the chin."

Gina rolled her eyes. "Maybe *you* should've married him."

"Don't be silly. I draw the line at men in their twenties. Now, give me a hot thirtysomething…"

"Mom." Gina made a cross with her two index fingers. "Way too much information."

Her mother, a vibrant and attractive fortysomething, smiled and took a sip of wine. "How about a glass of vino to get rid of those jitters?"

"I don't have jitters. I'm meeting a possible client for a drink." She grabbed her concealed-carry handbag with the special compartment for her .22 and hitched it over her shoulder.

"Oh, now he's a possible client? I thought this was purely social. Possible clients can see you at the office or arrange for a day of looking at houses."

"I'm looking at him as a possible client because I need to start building a business. I can't be Faith's gofer forever."

Mom leaned against the center island in the kitchen, cupping her wineglass with two hands. "Are you sure the real estate business is for you? I don't see much passion for it."

"It'll grow on me. I have to do something. I can't just tend bar. It's a dead end." Gina slipped into her high-heeled sandals, feeling a spark of excitement for the first time in a while.

"Get your own place going again. You did such a good job with that little Tex-Mex bar you had in Austin." Mom held up her hands. "I know you don't have the money, but I do. I could be your first investor."

"I can't do that, Mom. I can't take your money."

"Don't be ridiculous, Gina. Don't be proud. I earned that money."

"It's dirty money." Gina flung open the front door and slammed it behind her. She caught her breath and waited outside to make sure she hadn't woken up RJ.

Her mother called through the door. "He's still sleeping. Get a move on."

Gina blew out a breath and crossed the hall

to the elevator. Mom knew her too well. She'd been right about the nerves, too.

Josh Edwards's call hadn't surprised her too much. She'd felt the pull between them, had noticed the way he'd assessed her but wasn't sure he'd act on it. She wasn't sure she *wanted* him to act on it. Her trepidation had more to do with the fact that she didn't trust her instincts anymore rather than the fact that she hadn't dated since Ricky's assassination.

Maybe if she just pretended this was a work function, she wouldn't fall under Josh's spell. She'd keep her guard up and her .22 close.

The elevator landed in the lobby, and she crossed the marble tiles to the front door, waving at Enrique, the security guard at the desk.

Stepping into the night air of Miami, she inhaled the slightly sweet and spicy scent carried on a light breeze. She noticed this smell only here in South Beach—a combination of the perfumes and colognes of the women and men out for a night on the town and the savory odors from the restaurants lining the sidewalks and the occasional food truck hawking authentic Cuban food.

The bar she'd picked for her date with Josh got a good crowd on weeknights, but didn't command the standing room–only business of some other, more popular clubs. Cicero's would do for a quick drink and some informal chatter—that's all she could commit to right now.

She made a left turn at the corner and crossed the street. Squaring her shoulders and hugging her purse to her chest, she stepped into the bar and did a quick survey of the room.

Josh, sitting at a corner table facing the doorway, raised his hand.

Gina wove between the high cocktail tables until she reached the corner of the bar. As she approached, Josh stood up and grabbed her chair, holding it out for her.

Ricky had always done that, too—didn't mean a damned thing.

"Thank you." She scooted the chair closer to the table, hanging her purse over the back, gun compartment on the outside. "Have you been waiting long?"

"I got here about fifteen minutes early. You're right on time." He tapped the glass in front of him. "I just got some water, but I hope we see that waitress again. It's busy for a weeknight."

Gina turned an appraising eye on the scene—attractive waitresses, a good number of bartenders hustling up drinks and sharp busboys cleaning up tables as fast as customers vacated them. "Management's on the ball here. We won't wait long."

The waitress appeared at their table seconds later, as if she'd heard Gina's assessment. "Ready to order now?"

"I'd like a mojito, please. The house rum is fine."

"Sounds way too exotic for me. I'll have a beer, please. What do you have on tap?"

The waitress reeled off a list of beers from memory, and Josh selected an IPA.

Gina folded her hands on the table. "Have you given any more thought to that town house?"

"I might want to see a few more." Josh quirked an eyebrow at her. "Do you have any more to show me?"

"I can show you whatever you like." She bit her bottom lip. Did that sound like a come-on? She had to admit that Josh looked fine tonight—his short, almost black hair slicked back and a sexy scruff on his jaw.

She cleared her throat. "I mean, I can show you condos outside our own office's listings. Just tell me what you like."

His dark eyes glittered as they seemed to drill into her.

"I mean, tell me what you'd like to see…in a condo." She grabbed a menu tucked against the wall and skimmed the appetizers without seeing a thing.

Josh's intensity was off the charts up close and personal like this, face-to-face over a small table. With that stare burning a hole in her, anything she said sounded like a double entendre.

"I like that area. Maybe I'll make a list for you." Josh tapped the edge of the menu. "Do you want to order some food?"

"Not really." She blinked at the menu in her hands and then held it out to him. "Do you?"

"No, thanks."

The waitress saved her from any more inane conversation by delivering their drinks.

Gina poked at the mint leaves with her skinny green straw. "Where do you live now?"

"I'm new to Miami. I'm staying in a hotel not far from here." He took a sip from his beer, watching her over the rim of his mug.

Why did it seem as if they were having a conversation as a subtext to the words they were speaking? Every word from their lips felt loaded with meaning. Was it just this crazy attraction between them? She'd felt crazy attractions before—they never ended well.

If he could afford to stay in a hotel in South Beach long-term, he could afford a nice little town house just about anywhere in Miami.

She sucked up some of her drink and the cool mint tingled against her tongue. "Staying in a hotel must get...tiresome."

"There are certain advantages. I don't have to clean up after myself, or cook." He winked.

She studied his face. The wink didn't match the man. It was almost as if Josh was pretending to be someone he wasn't, or maybe she'd gone from not trusting her instincts to analyzing every word and every facial tick.

"How about you? I assumed you picked this bar because it was close to where you lived. Are you in South Beach?"

"We're temporarily staying with my mother, who has a condo here."

"We?" He casually curled a hand around his beer mug, but his knuckles appeared white.

She dragged her gaze away from his hand gripping the glass and met his dark eyes. Maybe he thought she was ready to spring a husband on him. Would a child be worse?

"My son and I. I have an almost three-year-old."

"That's great. Pictures?"

"Really? I don't want to bore you." Was this an act? Feign interest in the kid to get to the mom? Was this something men did? The last time she'd dated she didn't have a child, so this was new ground for her.

"Family pictures don't bore me."

Her fingers traced over the weapon stashed in her purse as she reached for her cell phone. Cupping it in her hand, she tapped her phone until she found a few current pictures of RJ.

"Here he is." She held the phone sideways in the middle of the table, so they could both see it. She had no intention of handing her phone over to him.

"Cute little guy."

She swept her finger to the next photo. "Here he is with his newfound friend from daycare."

Josh squinted at the picture. "They look like buds."

She pulled the phone back. "My son just started going to that daycare, so I'm happy he made such a fast friend."

The waitress dipped next to their table with two more drinks.

Josh glanced up. "We didn't order another round."

"I know." She slapped down a cocktail napkin and placed the second mojito on top of it. "A friend of yours at the bar ordered one for you."

Gina twisted her head to the left, her gaze tripping over the patrons at the bar. "I don't see anyone I know. Did she give her name?"

"*He* and no." The waitress shrugged and spun around to return to the bar.

Josh downed the rest of his first beer and pulled the second one toward him. "You have generous friends."

"Are you sure it's not one of your friends? I

don't see any of my friends at the bar, not that I have many here in Miami."

"I don't have any." He clinked his glass with hers. "Maybe it was a mistake. Should we drink up before he realizes it?"

One side of her mouth turned up in a smile, but she didn't feel like smiling. That was too weird. Who would be buying her drinks?

"Can you excuse me for a minute? I'm going to use the men's room." Josh shoved back from the table. "I'll swing by the bar to see if I recognize anyone."

"Maybe once this person sees you up close, he'll realize he made a mistake."

"You'd better take a sip of that drink before he can take it back."

As Josh walked toward the restrooms to the left of the bar, Gina picked up the second mojito and sniffed it.

A black scrawl on the cocktail napkin caught her eye and she dragged the napkin toward her with her index finger.

The words jumped out at her.

Dump this guy. You're still married. Meet me behind the bar down the block from Joanna's place, paloma. R.

Chapter Three

As he washed his hands, Josh leaned into the mirror and practiced winking. He was pretty sure that was a move his slick buddy Slade would've tried, but Gina had looked at him like she was staring into the face of Ted Bundy.

Maybe whoever sent that second round of drinks over noticed how badly he was tanking with Gina and was trying to help him out? That was a strange move for someone to make. If a friend of hers was at the bar, why not come by and introduce himself?

Maybe the guy was there right now and having better luck with Gina than he was. Could she be any more uptight? Maybe Ariel and her bunch had sent the wrong SEAL out here to do the job.

He yanked a couple of paper towels from the dispenser, dried his hands and tossed them into the trash before shoving out of the men's room. He held the door as two men came barreling through.

When he walked past the bar, nobody stopped him to claim responsibility for the drinks. He approached the table and sat down. Gina greeted him with a tight smile, her purse clutched in her lap, the second mojito untouched.

"Everything okay?"

"No, actually." She folded over the corner of the damp napkin beneath her empty glass. "I just got a call from my mom, and my son isn't feeling well. He woke up, and he's asking for me. I'm sorry. I'm going to have to leave now."

He watched her lips as they formed the lie.

"That's too bad. I hope it's nothing serious."

"Just a stomachache, but he needs his mom."

"Of course."

"I can leave some cash for my drink."

"I've got this one." He stood up as she shot up from her chair. "Can I walk you back to your mother's place?"

"No, thanks. It's not far and it's still crowded outside. I'll be fine." She stuffed a white napkin into her purse. "W-we could try this again...if you want, later."

"Sure. I'll make my list of requirements first—so we'll have something to talk about next time."

The zinger seemed to go over her head. "Fine,

yes. Call me." She pivoted toward the front door and practically leaped over the tables to get there.

As soon as she disappeared, Josh tossed some bills on the table and set Gina's full glass on top of them, since her second mojito seemed to be missing its cocktail napkin.

He'd seen a back door to the bar by the restrooms and made a beeline to that hallway. He slipped through the door and jogged toward the alley that led to the street. He flattened himself against the stucco wall and peered around the corner.

As he expected, Gina had already passed the alley. Her white jeans stood out in the crowd. *She* stood out in the crowd.

He joined the stream of people on the sidewalk, edging toward the curb, keeping cover. She glanced over her shoulder once or twice, but each time he stepped off the curb into the gutter and out of her view.

She turned and crossed the street, and he jaywalked to get out of her line of sight. He edged around the corner and spotted her several feet ahead of him.

Maybe she'd been telling the truth about her son. Her pale face and wide eyes when he'd returned to the table screamed *scared rabbit*, but maybe that's how she looked when her son was sick. Hell, what did he know about having kids?

Her mother's pastel-colored condo loomed down the block, and he'd have to end his sleuthing once Gina went inside. He'd probably never find out the truth about why she ditched the date early. It was probably that wink of his.

Then she passed the front entrance to the condo and his heart rate picked up. She wasn't going home to check on her sick child?

With one final twist of her head, Gina ducked into what looked like a bar almost a block down from her mother's condo. *Hello.* Maybe she wanted to pick up some ginger ale for the kid's stomach.

He didn't plan to blow his cover now by barging into the bar after her, so he cut down a small side street after the condo and headed to the alley running behind the buildings, including that bar.

He strode down the alley toward the back of the establishment, hoping it had a rear entrance. As he reached a Dumpster, a vision in white jeans and a red top stepped into the alley from beneath the black-and-gold awning of the bar's back door. A yellow light spilled over Gina's form beneath the awning.

Josh jerked back and ducked behind the Dumpster. Luckily, the light bulb that had been screwed in above the Dumpster lay in shards at his feet. Even if Gina glanced this way, he'd be nothing more than a shadow in the night.

And glance, she did. Her head turned from side to side as she rested a hand on the purse pressed against the front of her body.

Josh crouched and waited. She waited. They both waited for something…or more likely someone.

A slight movement across the alley caught Josh's attention and he melted against the wall, watching beneath half-shuttered lids.

A man emerged from the darkness, creeping like a jungle cat in his all-black clothing, his focus pinned on Gina, still in the doorway of the bar.

Josh's muscles tensed and his finger twitched as if it were on a trigger. He remedied that by slipping his hand in his jacket pocket and gripping the gun nestled there.

Through narrowed eyes, Josh followed the man's silent approach toward Gina. Could she see him coming at her through the blackness of the alley? The only light past the condo building was shining right on Gina. Where were the other lights from the other businesses? Josh nudged a piece of broken bulb with the toe of his shoe. Was this light broken by design?

A thrill of adrenaline percolated through his veins, and he hunched forward.

Gina's head jerked back. She'd spotted him—the predator.

She threw out one hand and her voice carried in the enclosed space of the alley. "Where is he?"

The man's voice came back, too low-pitched for Josh to hear a response.

"Where?" Gina tossed her long hair over one shoulder, giving a good impression of a woman in charge—but Josh picked up the tremor in the single word.

Once again, Josh missed the guy's response, but he pointed to the end of the alley.

Did Gina know this man? Would she go off with him? Josh couldn't allow that without knowing the identity of the man first. Somewhere in his job description for this assignment he'd read the word *protect*.

Gina shuffled forward without much enthusiasm, or at least not enough for her companion, who took her arm.

Wrong move, buddy. She shook him off and stepped back. "He can come here."

"He can't."

This time Josh heard him loud and clear.

"That's the only way." Gina shifted her stance

toward the door, but the man was beside her in a second, his hand on her shoulder.

She twisted away from him and that's all Josh had to see.

He stepped out from behind the Dumpster and startled a cat who'd been crouching and watching, too. The cat yowled in protest at being outed from his hiding place, and two white ovals in the night turned toward Josh.

Josh took one step forward and that was enough for Gina's pal. He shoved Gina against the door where she stumbled and went to her knees.

"Hey!" Josh took off, but the man was anticipating his move.

He spun around and sprinted down the alley.

Josh ran up to Gina. "Are you all right?"

"What are you doing here?"

"I'm going after him."

"No!" She grabbed the sleeve of his jacket, but he slipped away and chased after the man who'd reached the end of the alley and a cross street.

Josh pumped his legs to catch up, but a white sedan squealed to a stop and the man jumped into the back seat. Josh sprinted to the end of the alley and tried to get the license plate of the car, but it had already woven into traffic and all he could see was a white blur sandwiched between two other cars and a bus.

Josh spit out an expletive and dived back into the alley. When he reached Gina, she'd pulled herself up and was brushing dirt from her white jeans.

"What the hell are you doing here? Did you follow me?"

"It's a good thing I did." He jerked his thumb over his shoulder. "What was that all about? Did you know that guy?"

She backed up against the door, pinning her shoulders against it. "Are you some kind of creepy stalker? Was it you who closed the blinds and the door of the condo yesterday? I should've shot you when I had the chance." She patted her purse. "And I still might."

"Me?" He jabbed an index finger into his chest. "What about that guy? Was he, or was he not trying to get you to go somewhere with him."

She blinked and brushed some hair from her eyes. "I suppose so, but he was trying to take me to someone I know…knew."

"Don't you think that's suspicious? Why didn't the person just come to you?"

"That's what I was telling him when you appeared out of the shadows like some kind of night crawler."

"Thanks for that visual." He dragged his fingers through his hair. "And you weren't *telling* him that. You'd already told him and it didn't look like he was taking no for an answer, and then when I showed up like a *night crawler*, the dude pushed you and I'm the creep?"

"I didn't say he wasn't a creep, too."

Josh closed his eyes for a second and took a deep breath. "Are you going to tell me what that was all about?"

"Why should I?" She jutted her chin forward in a manner that told him she was ready for a long siege.

"Oh, I don't know, because we were on a date and you lied to me to get away and meet some creep in an alley. I figure you owe me an explanation. I even bought the drinks."

She sagged against the door, her once-proud shoulders slumped forward. "He said he could take me to my husband."

Josh's mouth dropped open. If she really thought Ricky Rojas was alive and well and living in Miami, he had some really bad news for her.

GINA FLINCHED AT Josh's expression of shock. If they did have any chance at a normal, dating kind of relationship, she'd have to open up to him about her life at some point. She just didn't expect it to be in a dark alley with her hands stinging from a fall and this suspicion between them.

Josh cleared his throat. "You're married?"

"I—I don't know." She rubbed at a smudge of dirt on the thigh of her jeans. "It's a long story."

Josh reached across her and opened the metal door of the bar. "Let's have another drink and you can tell me all about it."

She poked her head into the bright hallway that led to the noise and conviviality of the bar, and it all seemed so normal. She'd never told anyone her story and it bubbled and hissed inside her like some malignant concoction. She might not want to tell Josh Edwards the whole sordid tale but eking out a little at a time just might ease the pressure.

"Why the hell not?" She swept past him into the bar and the door slammed behind him as he followed her.

They couldn't find a table, but two stools beckoned at the end of the curved mahogany bar and they claimed them.

Josh rapped his knuckles against the wood. "Beer, please, whatever's on draft. Do you want one of those minty things again?"

"I'll have what he's having." She planted her elbows on the bar, hooking her feet around the legs of the stool.

Josh didn't waste any time. He spun around on his stool, bumping her knees with his, and leaned toward her. "Let's start with the basics. Are you married or not?"

"I was married to RJ's father, but I thought he died over a year ago."

Josh's dark brows collided over his nose. "You *thought* he died?"

"Yes, but the scene was kind of chaotic at the time, and I never actually saw his dead body. I mean, I saw his body, but for all I know he could've been faking it. I was *told* he'd died."

"Why would someone tell you that if it weren't true?"

"There are reasons, and I can't get into those."

The bartender placed their beers in front of them and Josh absently clinked his mug against hers. "What makes you think he's alive now? Just because that violent individual in the alley told you so?"

"That's not all. There have been a couple of other signs…messages."

"From him?"

Her hand jerked at Josh's harsh tone, and the beer sloshed over the side of the glass and ran down her hand. She plucked a cocktail napkin from the artfully arranged stack and dabbed her knuckles.

"A couple of texts using a...nickname that nobody else would know."

Josh leaned back and took a gulp of beer. "Why would your husband text you? Why not call you or better yet, walk up to your mother's place and knock on the door?"

She flicked the beer mug with her fingernail. How much should she reveal to this man she'd just met yesterday? Telling him the whole truth, that her husband and father had been involved in the drug trade and both had been killed at the same time in a planned assassination—would make anyone run for the exit.

That's not something you just blurted out on a first date.

"It's complicated, Josh. He wouldn't be in a position to just come to me freely."

"Sounds...dangerous."

"It is." She twisted her hair around one hand and then dropped it as the strands abraded the scrapes on her palm. "That's why I don't want to drag you into it from your safe and sane world of software development."

"Yeah, safe and sane." His lips quirked. "Sounds pretty far-fetched to me. Would you really go off with a stranger in search of your husband? Or did you know that man in the alley?"

"Never saw him before in my life."

Josh shook his head. "I can't believe a savvy

woman like you, a cautious woman like you, one who carries a .22 in her handbag on a date…"

She touched the purse hanging over her knee.

"Yeah, I know you have it in there. Anyway, can't believe someone like you would traipse off with a stranger promising to take you to your dead husband."

"I…" She pressed two fingers against her lips. She knew she'd been taking a risk meeting that man in the alley, but she had to know if Ricky was alive. "You're right, but he offered a compelling lure."

"That's exactly what it sounds like to me—a lure. That man in the alley wants something from you and figured the best way to get you to go with him was the story about your dead husband."

Hunching forward, she grabbed his wrist. "But what if it isn't a story? What if RJ's father is alive? I have to know."

"Forget about it, Gina. He's dead."

She flung his arm away from her. "You don't know that. You don't know anything. I'm sorry I told you."

"Why, because you don't want to hear the truth?"

"It's a possibility. Don't you understand that? I have to know for sure, for RJ's sake."

"He's dead, Gina."

"Stop saying that. How can you be so sure after hearing just a portion of the whole story?"

"I *am* sure."

"Why?"

"Because I was there when your father and husband were shot and killed."

Chapter Four

Ice water raced through her veins. She gulped against the sensation of drowning, but the air never seemed to make it to her lungs. She sputtered and gasped.

The stranger across from her squeezed her knee. "Do you need some water?"

"Water?" She gurgled. Why would she need water when the stuff threatened to overwhelm her?

"Gina, are you okay? I'm sorry. I didn't mean to spring it on you like this."

"Spring what?" She pressed her hands to her face, her skin cool and clammy beneath her touch. "Who are you? What do you want from me? Have you been the one sending those texts?"

His lying eyes widened. "Texts? Someone's been sending you texts?"

She tried to hop off the stool but forgot her

feet were hooked around its legs, and she fell forward instead. His arms curled around her, breaking her fall as she landed against his chest.

"I've given you a shock." He gently lifted her from the stool and set her on wobbly legs. "A table opened up in the corner. Let's grab it."

She didn't want to grab anything with this man, but she couldn't seem to form a coherent thought, never mind launch some kind of offensive against him.

She allowed him to lead her to the table and she plopped down in the chair.

He placed her mug of beer in front of her. "Have a drink."

Wrapping her hands around the heavy glass, she raised it to her lips and gulped down half the mug. Then she wiped the foam from her mouth with the back of her hand.

"Are you going to tell me who you are or am I going to whip that weapon out of my purse for encouragement?"

He had the nerve to smile, if that's what that twist of his lips meant.

"I'm glad to see you're coming around. You had me worried there for a minute."

"Stop stalling, Josh Edwards, or whoever you are."

"Josh Elliott—only a partial lie."

She ignored the hand he held out to her. "That

doesn't tell me a thing. *What* are you and why are you stalking me and how do you know about my father and my husband and how they died?"

"I'm a United States navy SEAL." He pulled out a wallet and snapped an ID card on the table between them.

Pressing her lips into a line, she poked it with her finger as if it could bite her. It looked official, but she knew all too well anything could be faked or forged. "And?"

"We assisted the CIA in Colombia when they took down the controlling members of the Los Santos drug cartel and the two terrorists they were meeting."

She flinched, nearly biting her tongue. "Terrorists?"

"The two men your father was meeting with that day—known terrorists."

The ice in her veins turned to molten lava as rage coursed through her system. "My father was meeting with terrorists in his home, while I was there? While RJ was there?"

"Afraid so." He cocked his head at her.

He didn't believe she didn't know.

"How did you assist the CIA? I didn't see any military there that day."

He blinked once, his spiky black lashes falling over dark eyes filled with secrets. "That's classified information. Let's just say we were there for protection."

"Not mine."

"Did the CIA…rough you up?" His jaw tightened.

"Did they pull out my fingernails under a bright bulb? Not quite, but it was no picnic, and the DEA was even worse."

"I'm sure it was…traumatic to lose your father and husband in that manner."

She flicked her fingers. "That was then. This is now. What are you doing here?"

"I'm here to protect you."

She snorted. "From what?"

"From that man in the alley who pretended he was going to take you to your dead husband." He steepled his blunt fingers. "From whomever is sending you text messages."

The worry she'd been experiencing ever since she'd received that first text washed over her once again, and she clutched her stomach. The sudden pain in her gut could be from mixing mojitos and beer, but she didn't think so.

"Ricky really isn't alive?"

"No way."

She took a slow sip of beer this time and licked the nutty taste from her lips as she considered this latest piece of news. Would this navy SEAL have any reason to lie to her... about this?

"I still don't understand. Why am I in danger all of a sudden?"

Folding his arms on the table, he lifted his chin. "Why don't you tell me what was in those texts?"

She dug her cell phone from her purse and skimmed through her messages. She stopped at the first one she'd received and read it aloud. "'Where are the drugs? Where are the weapons, *paloma*?'"

"*Paloma?* Dove."

"I-it was Ricky's nickname for me. *Nobody* knew about that name. That's why I believed that man tonight when he said Ricky was alive."

"I wouldn't put much stock in that. Ricky could've told anyone about it. Drugs and weapons? What do you know about drugs and weapons?"

She jerked back, putting more space between her and Josh's intense gaze. He might be here to protect her, but he didn't trust her.

She didn't trust him either.

"I don't know anything about drugs or weapons. I had nothing to do with my father's business and didn't even know his business until shortly before I was married."

"Once you knew his business and your husband's was drugs, why would you choose to put your son in danger by bringing him to that house?"

Gina crossed her arms, digging her fingernails into her biceps through the material of her silk blouse. She locked eyes with Josh, but this time the passion that kindled between them was anger, not sexual attraction.

She let a long breath out between her teeth that turned into a hiss. "It's complicated."

"And the other texts?" He sank back in his chair and sipped his beer.

"Same exact words, except the last message I received in the bar when you were in the restroom." She pulled a crumpled napkin from her purse and flattened in out on the table in front of him.

"Clever. He must've been the one who bought us the drinks."

She dropped the phone on top of the cocktail napkin. "My father was a drug dealer. I don't know anything about weapons."

"Do you want me to tell you?"

"Why wouldn't I?"

"I'm not sure you want to know the truth."

"Bring it."

"Your father, and the Los Santos cartel, had started dealing with terrorists out of Afghanistan. In exchange for the product from their poppy fields, he was going to supply them with weapons…and passage into the US."

Now she did feel sick.

She bent forward, leaning her forehead against the sticky table, her hair falling around her face. "I can't believe he'd do something like that."

And then she remembered what he'd done to her and she *could* believe it.

"Gina? Are you all right?"

Balancing her chin on the table, she peered at him through the curtain of her hair. "Not really. I thought this was all behind me."

"Can you think of any reason why your father's associates would be contacting you?"

"Is that who you think it is?" She blew the hair out of her face, as she raised her head.

"That's a good possibility."

"Could it be the Feds?" She splayed her hands on the table, wiggling her fingers. "Maybe they're trying to trap me?"

"I think I would've been told, since essentially I'm reporting to the Feds."

"The FBI? DEA? You're working with them?"

"What did you say before?" He rubbed his knuckles across the stubble on his jaw. "It's complicated."

"But what you're telling me is that if it was some federal agency trying to trap me, they wouldn't have sent you out here to protect me from that agency."

"Exactly." He placed his hands over her restless fingers. "I'm going to ask you a couple of questions. Can you try not to go off on me? I'm just asking."

Her gaze shifted to his broad hands covering hers. God, his touch felt good—warm, secure. She nodded. "I won't go off on you."

"Is there any reason why these people would think you know something about your father's business? Did he give you any information? Leave anything to you?"

"There wasn't much left." She slipped her hands from beneath his. Unless you counted the bank account on Isla Perdida. The same type of account her father had set up for her mother when they split, the one Mom had been using ever since to fund her lifestyle. Blood money.

"They seized all his assets…and mine."

"I'm sorry about that." He drummed his fingers against his glass. "They must think you know something. They wouldn't contact you, otherwise."

"They're sadly mistaken. Do you think I'm in danger from them?"

"You could be." Sounding casual, Josh lifted his shoulders, but they were stiff, indicating anything but casual.

"Great." She pushed away the mug of beer. "What was your original assignment? Get close to the grieving widow? Why the pretended interest in the property? Why not just approach me?"

His gaze floated over her left shoulder and she wondered if he'd heard her. Then his attention snapped back to her face. "I thought it might be better to get to know you in a non-threatening way first. I did shock you with all these revelations, didn't I?"

"Partly because I thought you were a mild-mannered programmer." Although there'd been nothing to suggest Josh Edwards/Elliott was mild mannered in any way, shape or form—her gaze skimmed over the powerful muscles on display beneath his shirt—especially form.

"My instructions were to get close to you." He cleared his throat. "This is a new type of assignment for me, so I wasn't sure about the best approach."

His lips twisted into a half smile, and her gaze lingered on his strong jaw imagining for a second what it would feel like to get close to Josh Elliott. Then she flipped her hair over her shoulder and said, "Honesty?"

"What?" The hand holding his beer mug jerked, and the amber liquid sloshed into small waves.

"I said you could've tried honesty in approaching me."

He curled his hands around the heavy, beveled glass and stared into its depths. "You really would've been open to a navy SEAL on a secret assignment appearing on your doorstep?"

"It's not like you were personally responsible for the deaths of my father and husband." She rolled her shoulders. "Besides, I accepted you when you did tell me the truth, didn't I? I mean, we're sitting here sharing a beer."

He held up one finger. "Ah, that's because I saved you in the alley, and you were still shaken up. I'm not sure you would've been so...accepting otherwise."

She screwed up her mouth and didn't bother refuting him. The man in the alley *had* shaken her up and she hadn't appreciated Josh's intervention at the time. Now that she knew Ricky really was dead, she was grateful for his protection. This might be a new type of assignment for him, but he'd caught on quickly.

Digging her elbow into the table, she buried her chin in one palm. "How exactly did the Navy SEALs fit into the raid on my father's place?"

"I can't talk about that."

"Okay, top secret." She tapped her fingertips against her cheekbone. "What now?"

"Keep your eyes and ears open, and be careful. I'll be here to look out for you until we can figure out why your father's associates are trying to contact you."

"If they tell me anything, I'll be sure to pass it along to you."

His dark eyes narrowed. "Tell you anything? Why and how would they have the opportunity to tell you anything?"

As she studied his glittering eyes, a chill touched her spine. In that instant she had an odd sense that she was staring into Ricky's eyes again. Josh's expression contained that same single-minded ferocity that Ricky had, but surely, Josh had a passion for good and justice, not evil and greed.

"I mean, if they text me again or, God forbid, call me since they seem to have my cell phone number."

Josh leveled a finger at her. "You're not going to run off and meet anyone again, are you?"

"No. I just thought…" She glanced down and studied her fingernails as she trailed off.

"Ricky's dead, Gina."

"I know." A single tear puddled in her right eye. Ricky had died a long time ago.

Josh slouched back in his chair and downed the rest of his beer. "Are you ready?"

She tapped her phone to wake it up, and the

numbers of the clock glowed in the dark bar. "My mom's going to think I had one hot date."

"If you want her to think that, you need to take a couple of deep breaths. Your face looks—" he touched a finger to her cheek "—tight."

His fingertip seemed to scorch her, to brand her. She sucked in a breath, and then shook her head. He was right. The events of the evening had taken their toll on her. The fear still had her senses buzzing.

"With any luck, my mother will be sound asleep and not lying in wait to ask nosy questions."

"Did your mother have any contact with your father after the divorce?"

"Divorce?" She dropped her phone into her purse. "Your sources aren't very well-informed. My mother and father never divorced, but they had very little contact after the separation."

"Did they separate after she discovered his business, or did she know his line of work before they married?"

"Top secret." Her lips formed a thin line, and she dragged her finger across the seam. If Josh, and the US government, didn't know the details of her parents' lives, she sure wasn't going to inform them.

She still had to protect her mom.

Clasping her purse to her body, she pushed up from the chair. "I'm ready to go."

Josh hopped up beside her and placed his hand at the small of her back to guide her out of the still-crowded bar. They spilled onto the sidewalk, joining the rest of the late-night revelers, stragglers from spring breaks across the country and snowbirds escaping the last ravages of winter in the Northeast.

A few steps later, and a popping noise had the press of people scattering and yelping in confusion.

Gina tripped over a crack in the sidewalk and stumbled off the curb. The cars in the street honked, as people surged into the road from the sidewalk to escape the firecrackers.

As Gina stood on her tiptoes to find Josh, she noticed from the corner of her eye a car peel away from the curb where it had been illegally parked. She turned toward the white sedan, and the back door flew open. A man lurched into the street and made a beeline for her.

Taking a step backward, Gina bumped into someone who wouldn't budge. She put a hand out. "Excuse me."

"Stop pushing, lady. Somebody's gonna get hurt."

"Yeah, me." She twisted her head back around, and the man from the car was an arm's length away.

Gina shifted sideways, but the man anticipated the move.

His fat fingers clamped around her upper arm and he almost lifted her from her feet as he dragged her toward the sedan.

She dug her heels into the asphalt. She was no match for him, but Josh was.

"Josh! Josh!"

As they got to the open door of the car, Gina grabbed onto the door frame. The big man peeled her fingers from the metal and twisted them back. She screamed amid another flurry of pops.

It was the driver of the car who'd been tossing firecrackers out the window.

Her abductor gave her a hard push from behind, and she fell face forward across the leather seats.

The man from the front seat growled, "Welcome back, Mrs. Rojas."

Chapter Five

The firecrackers were some sort of diversion. Josh craned his neck just in time to see Gina carried into the street by a sea of people.

He swallowed hard and plowed his way through the panicked pedestrians, losing sight of Gina in the process. A big white sedan, the same one that had carried away her assailant in the alley, blocked his view of the rest of the street and when he saw a large man at the open door, Josh's heart slammed against his chest.

He pushed a few people out of his way, and then jumped on the trunk of the car, sliding to the other side.

The big man was stuffing Gina into the back seat of the car.

Josh drew back his fist and landed it against the side of the man's head. The man stumbled back and Josh shouted, "Get out of the car, Gina!"

Encouraged by a pair of legs in white denim

that appeared in the doorway, Josh went at the big man again who was quickly regaining his composure and reaching into his pocket.

This bunch didn't want a dead body in the street any more than he did, but the big guy would probably make an exception for him. Josh charged the man, which felt like running into a brick wall. He grabbed the man's arm, twisting it behind his formidable bulk in one fluid movement.

The guy grunted and Josh continued to apply pressure until the man dropped to his knees. The driver began to get out of the car, but the whoop of sirens stopped him in his tracks.

Josh kicked the man's fat gut before leaping over his body and making his way back to the sidewalk. The whole attack took seconds, and the cops were rolling in for crowd control.

The squeal of tires told him the men in the sedan weren't going to stick around to answer questions about why they were tossing firecrackers onto a crowded sidewalk.

Josh's gaze swept up and down the street. Had Gina run to her mother's building? He squinted toward the purple awning, hoping to see her waiting there for him.

When someone wrapped an arm around him from behind, he spun around, fist clenched.

Gina held up one hand. "It's just me."

Warm relief rushed through his body and he pulled her into his arms. It's what he'd been wanting to do all night anyway.

"Are you all right? That big guy wasn't the same one from the alley."

"No, but I think the driver was the same guy."

He rubbed his hands up and down her arms. "Did he hurt you?"

"Just my fingers." She shook out her hand. "They really want me to go with them, don't they?"

"They sure do. They were behind the firecrackers. They wanted to create a panic and separate us."

"It worked. I nearly got trampled in the street. Before they drove off, I tried to get a license plate but there was no plate on the car."

"They'd never allow themselves to be traced through something like a license plate. Even if the car had one, it would've been stolen." He squeezed her shoulders before releasing her. "But good thinking."

"Maybe I should've just gone with them."

"What?" That was *not* good thinking. "Are you crazy?"

"Maybe they'd just tell me what they want and I could tell them I didn't have it, and they'd leave me alone." She chewed on her bottom lip.

"You know that's ridiculous, don't you? You

already know what they want. They texted that to you—drugs and weapons. And you already told them you don't know anything. Do you think they believe you?"

"I don't know." She tucked her fingertips into the front pockets of her jeans, crossing one leg over the other where she stood. "I didn't recognize those two tonight, but some of these guys have to be past associates of my father. Maybe I can reason with a couple of them."

"You don't follow the news much, do you?"

"What do you mean?"

"Does it look like the drug cartels are big fans of reasoning with anyone?"

"But my father…"

Josh sliced his hand through the air to stop her. "Your father was a vicious killer getting ready to deal with terrorists."

Her face blanched and her eyes glimmered like dark pools.

Anger bubbled in his blood. Didn't Gina realize by now that the company you kept could get you killed? How could she have ever married a man like Ricky Rojas, a member of her father's cartel?

Look what had happened to his own mother.

A shaft of pain pierced his temple and he massaged it with two fingers. "Let's get you home."

She shuffled her feet like a zombie as he

walked her to the entrance of her mother's building. He hadn't meant to hurt her, but maybe someone should've shocked her out of her naïveté long ago.

Or was it something other than naïveté?

Ariel, his contact for the assignment, had indicated that not only was he supposed to protect Gina De Santos but find out if she knew anything. Maybe she did know something. Maybe that's why she wanted to meet with her father's associates. He'd have to keep an eye on her.

As he glanced down at her wavy dark hair dancing around her shoulders and the curve of her hips in those tight jeans, he had a thoroughly primal male response. He wouldn't have any problem keeping an eye on Gina.

She turned at the doorway of the building. "Do you want me to call you when I hear something, or what?"

"Is this place secure?" He tipped his chin toward the pink art deco building with its purple-striped awning.

De Santos must've laid quite a settlement on his ex. That's probably why they didn't do the split legally.

"It's a safe building, and my mom has additional security, cameras. I'll be fine here."

"Touch base with me tomorrow if anything happens. Are you going to work?"

"Of course."

Her quick glance encompassed the luxury condo. "I have to make a living and support my son, even if I'm not sure realty is my thing."

He took her hand and smoothed the pad of his thumb over her knuckles. Guilt had been nibbling at the edges of his conscience ever since he snapped at her. He didn't know her story, didn't know what demons had pushed her into the arms of a drug dealer.

"Be careful and please don't meet with these people. They don't love you like I'm sure your father did, for all his faults."

An explosive little sob burst from her lips and she stabbed the buttons of the security keypad for the door. With one foot inside the ornate lobby, she twisted her head over her left shoulder. "I'll keep you posted, SEAL."

Josh watched her through the glass as she sauntered to the elevator. She flicked her fingers over her shoulder, and a flash of heat claimed his chest. He hadn't been as subtle in his... admiration as he thought if she knew he was watching her like a boy with his nose pressed against the candy case.

Josh blew out a breath and turned on his heel, diving back into the press of people still hopping from bar to club to bar. As he floated through and among the crowd, he felt as if he inhabited his own private island apart from the rest. These people had no idea about the danger that lurked in their presence. But he knew.

His teammates and superiors always tried to tell him he couldn't protect the entire world. But right now he'd be happy if he could protect just one woman.

THE FOLLOWING MORNING, Josh rose early to work out in the hotel gym and eat at the hotel restaurant. Then he settled in his room with his laptop whirring to life in front of him.

Drumming his thumbs on the keyboard, he gazed out his window onto the roof of another hotel. He had to compose a report to Ariel relaying the developments of last night without allowing his own suspicions of Gina to bleed into his words.

He dug his fingers into his scalp as he clutched his head. And what *were* his suspicions of Gina?

She seemed genuinely upset at the deaths of her father and husband. She'd seemed desperate to reconnect with Ricky Rojas. And she had secrets in her eyes.

Did she know something about the drugs and weapons? The DEA had originally thought so and had questioned her accordingly. They didn't break her, though.

Something told him Gina wouldn't break easily. He flexed his fingers and began typing his message to Ariel. He stuck to the facts and kept his opinions to himself. He didn't even know if the men who'd tried to abduct Gina were from the cartel or the terrorist cell—or both.

When he finished his report, he clicked Send and heaved out a sigh. He never much liked paperwork, but he had to furnish one of these reports every day to Ariel—whoever that was. The name sounded female, but he couldn't even count on that. This assignment reached the upper echelons of power, and the people pulling the strings had tightened security to a suffocating degree. He had a few contacts in Miami for outside help and support, but Ariel expected him to manage this mission on his own, creating as few waves as possible.

He shoved aside the secure, encrypted laptop and powered on his personal one. He did still have a life outside this assignment and planned to take advantage of being back on US soil.

His sniper team unit was somewhere on the other side of the world right now, but two of his team members, Austin and Slade, had already fulfilled missions for Ariel and her covert bunch. His team had been singled out specifically because of their connection to Vlad, a sniper for the other side. Had Vlad really grown so powerful that he'd been able to assemble a band of terrorists with worldwide connections? Austin and Slade had been convinced of it.

Josh scrolled through his email and stuttered over one from the NYPD. He double-clicked on it and hissed through his teeth when he saw Detective Potts's name at the bottom of it.

Dragging his finger across the text, Josh read every word of the message and pumped his fist when he reached the end. He'd hit pay dirt with Potts, the new detective for cold cases in the fifty-second precinct.

Potts had reopened his mother's case and had come across some information that hadn't been investigated previously. He wanted to meet with Josh.

Too bad the detective hadn't let him know sooner—like when he'd been in New York a few weeks ago assisting Slade with his…disposal problem.

He responded to Potts, letting him know he was in Miami for a few weeks, but would tell him if he made it to New York again. Josh slumped back in his chair and scuffed his knuckles across his jaw. Would it be a few weeks? How long would it take to protect and secure Gina De Santos…or find out what she was hiding?

If this assignment went well, his superiors

in the navy would have to give him a couple of days leave before he deployed. He'd spend them meeting with Potts in New York.

He skimmed through the rest of his emails, deleting more than he read.

As he closed the lid on his personal laptop, he eyed the file he'd been provided on Gina. He thought he knew her story but after meeting her, he couldn't figure out why a woman like her would give a punk like Rojas the time of day. He swept the file from the table and settled on the bed after punching a few pillows into submission.

He flipped open the file and scanned the details of her life. Her age surprised him. She seemed older than her twenty-six years, maybe because she'd been through a lot already—and had more coming her way.

He stared at the date she'd married Rojas, the birthdate of her son and the date of the day she'd become a widow, although he already had that date drilled into his memory. But those cold, hard facts didn't do a thing to explain why she'd married Rojas at the age of twenty-two or why she'd stayed with him as he climbed the ladder of the cartel.

She'd met him right after college, but the file didn't specify where. They'd opened a bar together a year later and had a son shortly after that.

He tossed the file off the bed with a grunt of disgust. Probably opened the bar with drug money and laundered it there. That had to be why the government took the place after the... assassinations.

She'd lost everything, and he'd been partially responsible for that.

He leaned over the side of the bed and gathered up the photos that had fanned out from the file. The first pictures showed Gina after the hits on her father and his associates, including her husband.

Josh squinted at the images. Gina seemed strangely detached. While everyone else scurried around in shock and terror, she comforted them. She alone knew exactly what had happened and why.

The next few pictures showed her in the interrogation room, her face strained but not a teardrop in sight. Did her composure indicate shock and disbelief or did it mean a new opportunity had just opened up for her?

A female head of a cartel would be different—and tricky. Had she taken over where her father and husband had left off?

He stacked the photos and turned them over. He needed a bottle of water to get the sour taste out of his mouth.

He rolled off the bed and reached for the mini

fridge. As he twisted the cap off a water bottle, his phone buzzed.

Leaning against the window, he grabbed it from the table and swept his finger across the display to see the text message from Gina.

He read it aloud. "'I need to see you. I have something to confess.'"

Tapping the phone against his chin, he grimaced. If Gina De Santos thought she could play a New York street kid like him—she had another think coming.

Chapter Six

Gina pulled down the slat of the cheap blind at the window and squinted into the street. Her gun weighed down the purse strapped across her body, and she rested her hand lightly on the outside pocket that concealed it.

Two abduction attempts in one night called for extreme measures, although she couldn't help thinking if Josh hadn't come to the rescue that second time in the street, she might have this whole issue solved.

She'd lied to Josh about the driver of the sedan. She'd recognized his voice even though she'd been facedown in the back seat and couldn't see him. Pablo Guerrero had been one of her father's top lieutenants in the cartel. A bad cold had kept Guerrero home from the meeting the day her father and Ricky had been hit.

She'd given up his identity readily to the

DEA, but that hadn't impressed the agents. They knew all about Guerrero, and she'd suspected they might have even been working with him.

Guerrero obviously had plans to resurrect the Los Santos cartel with himself as kingpin, and he figured he could start with her and those missing drugs and weapons.

He'd always seemed like a reasonable guy, as far as drug dealers went. Maybe if she could just tell Guerrero she knew nothing, he'd leave her alone.

Of course, that would be a lie, and if she had to confess anything she'd rather do it to the hot navy SEAL who was the good guy in all this than a drug dealer looking to make fat stacks off other people's misery.

It had been a long time since she'd met a good guy.

Her heart stuttered when the silver compact wheeled in front of the house she'd told Faith she was showing to a prospective buyer. In fact, she was becoming quite the accomplished liar—must come from years of lying to herself.

Josh emerged from the driver's side, took a quick look up and down the street and strode up the driveway with a purpose that had her re-thinking her decision.

He already didn't trust her. Why would he? The daughter and wife of drug dealers, who'd stayed even after she learned the truth about both. She would never be able to explain it to him. A man like that had control of every aspect of his life.

When he knocked on the front door, she huffed out a breath, misting a spot on the window before reaching for the door handle.

She threw open the door and stepped to the side. "Thanks for coming."

"How could I refuse to respond to a text like that? A confession?"

"Well, maybe I was being a little dramatic." She ducked her head.

"Everything about you has been dramatic from the moment I…met you." He locked the door behind them. "Are you sure it's okay to meet here?"

"Why not?" She shrugged. "I was planning on showing this dump today anyway, but the people looking canceled out on me. My coworker was none the wiser."

He peeked through the blinds just as she had done a few minutes earlier. "You weren't followed, were you?"

"I paid attention. Believe me, after having the CIA, the FBI and the DEA breathing down my neck for the past year, I recognize a tail when I see one." She patted her purse. "And I'm packing heat."

He held up his hands. "You sure you know how to use that thing?"

"Didn't I prove it to you the last time we were alone in a house together?" Tipping her head to one side, she dropped her lids, studying him out of half-closed eyes. "Besides, don't you think I'm some kind of drug moll?"

Josh tilted his head back and laughed at the seventies' popcorn ceiling. "What the hell is a drug moll?"

A smile tugged at her lips. That dry laugh seemed more natural than the grins and the winks, and transformed Josh's too-serious, tense face, lighting it up and making him look almost boyish.

"You know, like the women who hang around gangsters, but in this case, drug dealers."

His laugh evaporated as suddenly as it had burst forth and reminded her that he really didn't trust her at all.

She hoped to remedy that. She wanted Josh Elliott to trust her, to like her.

"Anyway, what I meant to imply is that there's a good chance someone like me with a father like I had is going to know her way around a weapon—and I do."

"I believe you." He rubbed the back of his neck with one hand. "What is it you want to confess?"

She waved her hand toward the two stools at

the kitchen peninsula, the only pieces of furniture left in the house. "Can we sit?"

Josh straddled the stool from behind and crossed his arms over his leather jacket. "Okay."

Perching on the stool across from him, she swept her tongue across her bottom lip. "I haven't been completely honest with you…or my father's associates."

Josh's Adam's apple bobbed in his throat and his nostrils flared. "Go on."

"I don't know anything about drugs or weapons, but I do know something about offshore accounts." She held her breath.

Josh blinked. "Offshore accounts?"

"Are you familiar with Isla Perdida?" She waved a hand in the air. "Of course you are."

"The Caribbean island that doubles as a playground for the rich and famous and a hiding place for their money." He uncrossed his arms and wedged his hands on his knees. "Does your father have an account there?"

"He does."

"You were able to keep that from the DEA?"

"I was."

He whistled through his teeth and settled back, giving her some breathing room. "You're good."

"It's not for me." She bolted up straight, hooking her feet around the legs of the stool so she wouldn't fall into his lap…again. "I don't use any of that money."

"Who does?"

He narrowed his eyes, and she willed the heat creeping up from her chest to stay out of her face. Nothing like looking guilty when she wasn't—not really.

"That's how my father has been giving money to my mother for years. She has an accountant down there who facilitates everything."

Josh's eyelids drooped even more and she could almost believe he was asleep except for the way the muscles in his face twitched and shifted, as if his thoughts were running riot across his countenance.

"So, the ritzy condo in the ritzy building in the ritzy area…"

"Drug money."

"You're living there, living off that money."

"Not completely." She sucked in her lower lip and met Josh's hard stare. Who said confession was good for the soul? "When the US government seized all my assets—because Ricky's assets were mine and mine were his—I had no money, no property, nothing. I needed a place to stay and Mom offered. That's why I snatched at the first halfway decent job with career potential that popped up. I don't like selling real estate, but one of Mom's connections got me in and I need to make money so I can divorce myself from my mother and her blood money."

Josh cocked his head to one side, as if examining a rare bird.

"And why do you think this account in Isla Perdida is important? It sounds like it's money your father already made. Do you think it's enough to buy the weapons he planned to trade to the terrorists for their drugs?"

"Oh, no. I'm pretty sure that deal had already gone down before the CIA took him out. That's *why* the CIA took him out."

Josh shifted on his stool and raked a hand through his short hair. "That's what we figured, also."

"Then why did the CIA kill my father before they knew where he'd stashed the drugs from the terrorists and the weapons he intended to pass off to them in exchange?"

"We… They thought they did know. The CIA managed to get to your father's driver, Chico Fernandez and wire him up. Chico recorded a conversation between your father and…your husband in the car. He mentioned a location then, and the CIA thought that's where he'd stashed everything."

Tapping one fingernail on the counter, Gina said, "Chico disappeared a few weeks before my father was killed."

"We don't know anything about that. He disappeared off our radar, too."

"D-do you think Chico's dead?"

"Maybe. Maybe your father discovered the wire, or Chico decided to hightail it out of your father's employ before he *did* discover it."

She rubbed the goose bumps from her arms. Her father's savagery never failed to stun her—even though she knew its real depths more than anyone.

Josh's eyes flickered at the gesture. "If you already know the money for the deal is not in the offshore account, why do you think it's so important to bring it up now after keeping it a secret all this time?"

"Because my father has more than just an account there. He also keeps a safe-deposit box at the Banco de Perdida on the island."

"Big enough for a stash of weapons?" His mouth twitched.

"Of course not." She brushed a strand of hair from her face impatiently. "But Isla Perdida was my father's safe place, just as it is for a lot of criminals. If there was something he wanted to protect, some information he wanted to keep hidden, he'd store it there."

"Do you think he was planning to double-cross the terrorists he was dealing with?"

"I don't know. Maybe he could feel the trap

closing around him and took steps to avoid it. What I do know—" she leaned forward, almost touching her nose to his "—is that he went to Isla Perdida one week before the raid on his compound."

Josh shook his head. "No, he didn't. The CIA was watching his every move. He was in Bogotá that week."

Gina snorted. "That was Uncle Felipe."

"What?"

She pressed her lips into a neat smile. She got a certain satisfaction from his reaction—Mr. Know-It-All.

"Uncle Felipe, my father's brother, was his body double. My father used Felipe to throw off his enemies." She held up two fingers, side by side. "They were like this, only seventeen months apart, looked like twins."

"Felipe De Santos is in a Colombian jail right now, but he never said one word about the role he played in your father's organization."

"Why would he? My father had trained him long ago, even when they were children, to keep his mouth shut. He was a good soldier all those years."

"Except he wasn't at the house when the deal went down. Why?"

"My father never trusted him with important business." She tapped her head with one finger. "Always thought he was slow. He wasn't as clever as my father, but he wasn't slow. I guess his perceived dim-wittedness saved his life in the end."

"If I'm to believe you, your father sent Felipe to Bogotá to impersonate him while he staged a getaway to Isla Perdida one week before the raid."

"Yep, and I highly advise you to believe me. I have proof that he went."

"What proof?"

"A communication between him and his pilot. You don't think he hopped on a commercial jet, do you?"

"How did he manage to take a private jet out of the country?"

"How did Hector De Santos manage to do anything? Greased palms and payoffs." She clenched her jaw. "And threats."

"And you believe he went to Isla Perdida to protect information?"

"Yes. If the FBI, CIA and DEA can't find the drugs and weapons and if my father's own associates can't find them, he must've hidden them very, very well."

"I suppose if you give us the information about the account, the ops group I'm working with can go in and have a look."

"Uh-uh."

His brows shot up. "What?"

"I'm not giving them any information about that account, and I'll deny everything you tell them."

"Wait. I thought that's why you told me about the account."

"I told you about the account because I believe you might be able to find the information you're looking for, but that money belongs to my mother. I'm not allowing you or anyone else to take that away from her."

He spread his hands. "Then what are you proposing?"

"I'm proposing we do it my way."

"Which is?"

"We'll go down to Isla Perdida together."

Chapter Seven

The following day, Josh emptied the contents of his small bag into his big suitcase and dropped the empty bag on the bed. He'd reported to Ariel that he and Gina were taking a trip, but didn't mention the location.

When the truth came out that their jaunt had taken them to Isla Perdida, would it be enough to get him yanked off this assignment? His commanding officer in the navy had assured him nothing that happened on this assignment would impact his career as a navy SEAL—unless he died. That would impact it plenty.

Gina had been working all day while he finalized details of their trip tomorrow, and she'd be joining him for dinner in less than thirty minutes. Maybe they could have a real date tonight, free of suspicions and half-truths.

The half-truths would have to start back up tomorrow. They'd be traveling to Isla Perdida under assumed names, but Gina would have her ID on the island. She'd made another confession to him that she'd actually accompanied her father to Isla Perdida once, and he'd given her everything she needed to access his safe-deposit box.

Josh rolled up a T-shirt and tossed it into the bag. Why would her father have done that if she hadn't given him some indication she was willing to learn Los Santos's operations and had every intention of continuing her father's evil legacy? Maybe she'd been playing both sides. Maybe she was playing both sides now.

He packed a few more items and as he hauled the bag from the bed, a knock sounded at the door of his hotel room. He strode to the door and put his eye to the peephole. He opened the door for Gina and swallowed as he took in her red dress that hit just above her knee and hugged her in all the right places.

Maybe she wanted to have a real date, too.

"Are you early, or did I lose track of time?"

"I'm five minutes early." She took a turn around the room and kicked his bag with the toe of her high-heeled shoe, red to match her dress. "Are you all packed?"

"Pretty much. Are you?"

"Threw some things in a carry-on when I got home from work."

"How'd work go?" Josh glanced down at his jeans, rethinking his clothing choices for the evening.

"Not great." She tossed a wave of dark hair over her shoulder. "Faith wasn't thrilled that I was taking off for a few days. I think I'm going to lose this job."

He knew the feeling.

He slid back the closet door and yanked a pair of black slacks from a hanger. "Doesn't sound as if you much like it anyway."

"I don't, but what am I going to do, be a spy for the CIA?" She snorted.

"I'm going to change." He held up the slacks, pretending he was going to wear them all along. He slipped into the bathroom and pulled off the jeans. Good thing he hadn't worn the slacks yet and they were still pressed.

When he walked back into the room, his personal cell phone was ringing.

Gina handed it to him. "Just started."

As he took it from her, he glanced at the display and his pulse jumped. He tapped the phone to answer it. "Elliott."

"Mr. Elliott, it's Detective Potts. In your email you indicated that you were in Miami. Well, I had to come out here for a case, and I thought I could kill two birds with one stone. I'm still here if you're free tonight."

Josh glanced at Gina, her eyes wide and questioning. "It's not the best time right now, Detective."

"You've waited over twelve years for this information and now's not the right time?"

"You said you found some uninvestigated information."

"I must've sounded too casual, Mr. Elliott, because it's more than that."

"More?" Josh's mouth felt dry and he couldn't swallow, couldn't breathe.

"Mr. Elliott, I have a good idea who murdered your mother."

"You're kidding."

"I'm not. Do you want me to lay it out for you tonight? Or I'll be here most of tomorrow. I think I can swing a breakfast meeting."

"I'm leaving tomorrow and going out to dinner tonight. I can meet you…after dinner."

"Give me the name of the restaurant, and I'll join you for coffee. One thing you can say for Miami, the restaurants stay open as late as the ones in New York."

Josh's gaze darted toward Gina, who was still watching him, her head tilted to one side. He hadn't told Gina anything about his family, but then why would he? He knew all about her family because it was part of his job. He'd never told anyone the full story behind his mother's death—not even his navy SEAL team members.

He inhaled a deep breath and gave Detective Potts the name of the Cuban restaurant where he and Gina would be dining and told him to be there around ten o'clock.

As soon as he ended the call, Gina asked, "What was that about? Not our current situation?"

"Something personal. I'm sorry. I know the timing couldn't be worse. I don't want to ruin our dinner, but this meeting has to happen tonight."

She folded her hands in front of her. "Are you going to tell me what it's all about? You'll have to unless you plan to send me home after we eat. When you first answered the phone, I thought you were going to fall over, and I'm sure it would take a lot to make you fall over."

He didn't plan to send her away after dinner. "It's about my mother."

"Is she okay?"

"My mother died many years ago."

"I'm so sorry. The phone call…?"

Clearing his throat, he stashed his phone in the pocket of his slacks. "My mother was murdered."

Gina crossed her hands over her chest. "That's terrible. How old were you?"

"Sixteen."

"And your father?"

"Long gone before then."

"What happened?"

"I never really knew. She was shot in the back of the head in an alley."

Gina had been approaching him slowly from across the room and when she reached him, she placed a hand on his arm. "That must've been horrible for you."

He met her dark eyes and couldn't look away from the compassion that made them glow. All this mess was going on in her own life and she had feelings to spare for him?

"I want to help you, Josh, like you've helped me."

"Help me? You don't have to, and I don't even know that you can. I've been living with this hell for twelve years."

"You've been living with it by yourself, haven't you? Tell me about it. Unburden yourself. You might feel a little better." She shrugged. "I'm going to find out about it after dinner anyway. I'd rather hear it straight from you than...?"

"Detective Potts."

"Detective Potts."

"It's an ugly story." He picked up her hand from his arm and kissed the inside of her wrist. She took his hands and dragged him toward the bed. "Tell me about it, and tell me why you're meeting Potts tonight. Like you said, I was a little early and we have some time before our dinner reservation."

He sat beside her on the mattress while she kept possession of his hand, and he pinched the bridge of his nose. "My dad was out of my life by the time I was two and my brother, Jake, was four. My father was a junkie and my mom was, too."

Gina squeezed his hand but if she kept that up through all the sad parts of his story, she'd cut off his circulation after about ten minutes.

"Where's your brother now?"

"Prison."

She blinked a few times and then pressed her lips together.

"When my dad left, my mom waitressed and walked the streets a little to make ends meet—feed us and feed her drug habit. She was still doing drugs and part-time hooking by the time I was a teenager. How she managed to survive that long and keep custody of us is beyond me, but she did. Then her luck ran out."

"Was she killed by one of her...johns?"

"That's what the cops thought, but Jake had his own theory. He was sure Mom's murder had to do with the guy she'd been seeing, Joey O'Hanlon. Joey O disappeared after the murder. Jake kept trying to tell the police about him, but the cops had their narrative and they were sticking to it."

"Did they have any good reason to stay with their story?"

"One of the working girls on the street saw my mother walk away with a guy who'd been trolling, swore he was a regular john. The cops focused on him but never found him. Unsolved murder, cold case."

"What happened to your brother? Why is he in prison?"

"He found Joey, claimed he killed him in self-defense but had to take a plea for second-degree murder."

Gina shook her head. "That's just all kinds of messed up."

"But I'll never forget what Jake told me. He said before he and Joey struggled over the gun, Joey claimed that Mom was murdered over drugs."

"She was? Was she selling or dealing?"

"No, but Joey O was." Josh skimmed a hand over his short hair. "We tried to tell the police, but they wouldn't listen to us."

"So, you'd already lost your dad, you lost your mom to murder and you lost your older brother to prison."

"Told you it was a sad story."

She trailed a hand down his back and he shivered. "What does Potts have?"

"He thinks he knows the killer, after twelve years as a cold case."

"Then you absolutely have to meet with him, and I'll gladly give over our dessert and coffee time so you can get some closure."

"Closure. I guess we all need some of that." He kissed the tips of her fingers and pushed up from the mattress.

JOSH SURVEYED THE restaurant and was glad he'd changed clothes. Plenty of men were wearing jeans, but they'd paired them with silk shirts in bright hues, unbuttoned to create a V on their chests and adorned with several gold chains. Not his scene, but his black slacks and white shirt fit in with all the peacocks.

Gina had ordered a mojito again but he stuck with beer. Josh liked his food—and his women—spicy, so the Cuban dishes—and Gina—made his mouth water. They both ordered the *ropa vieja* and spent most of the meal talking about Isla Perdida and RJ.

"I feel so blessed that RJ is a happy boy, and he makes friends easily. We already had Diego, a little friend of his, over to Mom's for a playdate."

"Does he ask about his father?"

"Did you? You said your father was out of your life by the time you were two. RJ was about the same age."

Josh chased a kernel of rice around his plate with his fork. "I don't remember. I'm sure the questions didn't come until later, when I got to school and saw other kids with fathers. I think a boy will always miss a father figure in his life."

"Your mother never remarried?"

His lip curled. "She and my father weren't married and while she brought a lot of men around our apartment, she never married and I'd hardly call them father figures."

"RJ would look for his father, and his grandfather. He'd say their names. I tried to explain to him they were gone." She swirled her drink. "I don't know how much of that he took in. I'm gearing up for the questions later, and I honestly don't know how I'm going to answer them. How'd your mother handle it?"

Giving up on the rice, Josh stabbed a bean. "She told me and Jake that our father was a no-good bum and we were lucky he was out of our lives."

"That's one option." Gina pushed away her plate and asked a passing waitress for the dessert menu.

Rolling his wrist inward to check his watch,

Josh said, "It's almost ten. Potts will be just in time to join us for coffee."

They ordered a key lime pie to share and two cups of Cuban coffee. Halfway through the pie and two sips into the sweet brew, Josh noticed the waitress leading a short, broad African American man with graying hair to their table.

Josh jumped up from his chair and extended his hand. "Detective Potts?"

"Good to meet you, Mr. Elliott."

"Josh. You can call me Josh and this is Gina."

When he was finished shaking Josh's hand, Potts engulfed Gina's in his clasp. "I hate to interrupt your dinner like this, but it seems like we're both on tight schedules."

"I'm glad you made it down here. Do you want some coffee? Dessert?"

"I ordered a cup of Cuban from the waitress while she walked me over here."

Josh crumpled up his napkin and tossed it next to his plate. "You know the name of my mother's killer?"

"It's a little more complicated than that."

"Complicated? Did Joey O'Hanlon have one of his dirtbag pals do it? I know he had an alibi, but my brother always thought he was to blame."

"Your brother's up for parole in a year."

"You sayin' you can help with that?"

"I might be able to, but Joey wasn't the one

who ordered your mother's death, although he was indirectly responsible for it."

"I knew it."

"Joey O was a small-time drug dealer, which I'm sure you know by now. What you probably don't know is that Joey was stealing from his supplier, doing a little selling on his own."

"That's dangerous business."

"It's all dangerous business." Potts stopped talking and smiled his thanks at the waitress who delivered his coffee. He took a careful sip from the dainty cup. "Anyway, the supplier caught on and his boss caught on and so on and so on, and someone came out to pay Joey O a visit."

"He must've known what was coming down because he took off."

"That's right." Potts cradled the cup in his palm. "But your mother didn't. The hit man sent to take care of Joey couldn't find him, but he did find a substitute."

Josh's eye twitched. "Do you know the name of the hit man?"

"No, and we may never locate him, but we know who ordered the hit and you may get some satisfaction out of knowing that person is dead."

"Who was it? Who ordered the hit on my mother?"

"A big-time drug dealer—Hector De Santos."

Chapter Eight

Potts's words punched Josh in the gut but before he even had a second to react, Gina dropped her cup and it broke right in half, the dark liquid pooling in the saucer.

It was enough to distract Potts from Josh, giving him time to compose his features. So, he'd killed Gina's husband and her father had killed his mother…indirectly. A match made in heaven.

"Are you okay, ma'am?" Detective Potts reached across the table, picked up a piece of the cup and placed it in the saucer.

"I—I'm fine." Her face drained of all color, Gina grabbed her napkin and blotted up the drops of coffee dotting the table.

Josh coughed. "Hector De Santos. Isn't he the head of some big drug cartel?"

"He was. As I mentioned, he's dead now—no big loss."

"A guy like that was concerning himself with some small-time drug dealer in the Bronx?"

Potts spread his hands. "We all have to start somewhere. De Santos was still solidifying his empire twelve years ago, and that's one way he rose to power so quickly. He didn't mess around. You toyed with Hector De Santos, you paid the price."

"So, even if the NYPD back then had made this connection, there wasn't much they could've done about it. The triggerman was probably on his way back to Colombia within hours of murdering my mother."

"Could be and I'm sorry about that, but I thought you'd want some closure and I meant what I said about your brother, Jake. Tough rap for him when any one of us might've done the same thing to someone who'd wrecked our mothers' lives."

His mother had wrecked her life long before Joey O crashed onto the scene. "I appreciate the effort, Detective Potts."

"Allen." The detective pulled a card from his wallet and slid it across the table to Josh. "Let me know if you need anything and thank you for your service, chief."

The men shook hands, and the detective nodded at Gina as he pushed back from the table.

When Potts walked away, Gina folded her

hands on the table, an incredible stillness falling over her as if she were resting in the eye of a storm.

There would be no storm.

Josh dabbed at a crumb from the pie plate with the pad of his finger. When he caught it, he sucked it into his mouth, meeting Gina's gaze for the first time since Potts delivered the bombshell.

She blinked her long lashes once but held his stare. "You don't seem very surprised."

"To hear your father's name from the detective's lips?" He hunched his shoulders. "It threw me for a loop, but it kind of makes sense. It's like some perfect circle." Gina didn't realize how perfect a circle it was.

"I'm—I'm so…"

He held up a hand. "Don't tell me you're sorry. It's not your fault that your father was a drug dealer. It's what you do going forward that counts."

"I will do anything I can to help you, starting with Isla Perdida." She grabbed his hands. "Did it help seeing Potts? Did it give you that closure he mentioned?"

"It gave me…resolve."

THE NEXT DAY, Josh looked into the small, upturned face, dark eyes wide with curiosity, and cleared his throat. What were you supposed to say to a three-year-old? Was RJ too young to watch basketball? Too old for nursery rhymes?

RJ tugged on Josh's sleeve and pointed to a plastic truck on the floor.

"Is that your truck?" What a dumb question. Whose truck would it be? His mother's? His grandmother's?

RJ didn't seem to mind the stupid query as he nodded and smiled. He also tugged on Josh's sleeve again.

Josh dropped to his knees and placed a hand on top of the truck. He rolled it on the tile floor, and RJ scooted along beside it, tossing obstacles in its course. Josh dragged the toy over every magazine, coaster and pillow RJ put in the truck's way and even started making roaring truck noises in the process.

The heavy scent of musky perfume invaded his nostrils, and Josh twisted his head over his shoulder, his nose almost colliding with Joanna De Santos's kneecap.

She raised her penciled-in brows. "Getting to know RJ?"

"Just…uh—" he lifted the truck into the air, its wheels still spinning "—playing with the truck."

"You and Gina were awfully private about your dating. You've been seeing each other a few months and are ready to jet off on vacation together and this is the first time I'm even heard your name."

"Mom, I told you we wanted to keep things low-key." Breezing into the room, pulling a suitcase behind her, Gina nodded toward RJ, now constructing a full-scale obstacle course for the truck.

Joanna fluffed her dyed red hair around her shoulders. "When Gina told me you two were heading to the Bahamas together, I insisted that she introduce you to us before she left."

"A good idea and understandable." Josh crawled forward a few feet, pushing the truck ahead of him and aiming it at the tunnel RJ had created by propping up two cushions against each other.

"Yeah, well, Gina doesn't have the best taste in men."

"Mom!" Gina rolled her eyes at Josh. "This is exactly why I didn't bring him around. Would you please let me tell my own life story in my own way?"

"Sure, sure." Joanna flicked her long fingernails at Gina. "You two go off and have fun. God knows, you deserve it."

"Remember, just take RJ to his daycare like usual. I talked to the mother of Diego, his friend, about a playdate, so you can follow up with that. Remember, she brought him over here a few weeks ago." Gina leaned over and kissed her mother's cheek. "I'll text you when we get there, but let's not do any video chatting with RJ. I don't want him to be confused."

Crossing her arms, Joanna said, "Check, check, check."

Josh completed the obstacle course as RJ coached him. Then he ruffled the kid's hair and pushed to his feet just as Gina crouched down next to her son.

She touched noses with RJ before dragging him into her lap. "Be a good boy for Mami, and I'll bring you a present."

RJ curled his arms around Gina's neck and said, "Can I play with Diego?"

"I think so, and I won't be gone long so if Mami doesn't take you to Diego's, I will when I come back."

RJ cupped a hand over Gina's ear and whispered.

She smiled and kissed him. "I think he'd like that."

RJ jumped to his feet and scampered into the family room.

Earlier Josh had poked his head in that room, with its multitude of toys and a big-screen TV with beanbag chairs and game consoles—a little boy's paradise. Grandma must be footing the bill for that, too.

Two seconds later, RJ bolted out of the room, clutching something in his small hands. He raced to Josh, arms outstretched.

"Whaddya got there?"

"A truck." RJ opened his hands where a red truck balanced on his palms. "A toy for the airplane."

"Thanks, RJ. That's just what I need."

He heard a soft snort behind him. Joanna didn't trust him for some reason—not that she should, but they couldn't tell Gina's mother the truth. If Gina's mother knew who he was and what he'd done, she would be doing more than snorting at his back.

Gina came up behind her son and combed her fingers through his messy hair. "That was thoughtful of you, RJ. Now, give me a big kiss before I leave."

She scooped him up in her arms and they traded kisses back and forth.

Whatever else Ricky Rojas had done, he'd given Gina a son and she obviously didn't regret that. Did she regret anything about that marriage? She'd said very little about Rojas, and Josh hadn't wanted to encourage her in case it led to the truth of what had happened that day in Colombia. Even after Potts's revelation last night, Josh wasn't ready to reveal he'd been the one looking at Ricky through the scope.

"Are you sure you don't want me to drop you off at the airport?"

"No, Mom. We're good. Just take care of RJ."

"Of course."

Ten minutes later, they were clambering into a taxi, their bags in the back. Josh collapsed against the seat, feeling as if he'd just navigated through an obstacle course—just like that truck. "Your mom really didn't like me, did she?"

"She's just...protective of me."

"Protective?" Joanna's criticism of Gina had left a sour taste in his mouth—not that he didn't agree with it. "Your mother doesn't have much room to talk about bad taste in men."

"Mom's just speaking from experience." Gina poked him in the ribs and jerked her thumb toward the driver in the front.

Josh doubted the guy could hear one word they said, but he sealed his lips and spent most of the ride to the airport making sure they didn't have company on their way.

He wouldn't admit it to Gina, but the scariest part of that condo encounter was meeting RJ. Josh didn't have any children in his life and didn't have the first clue how to act with them, but RJ had gone easy on him.

The chaos in RJ's life had produced a seemingly well-adjusted, social kid. How had RJ escaped unscathed? Josh and his brother sure hadn't.

The taxi driver confirmed their airline with them and then navigated through the traffic of airport departures before pulling up to the curb.

They had their boarding passes and carry-on luggage only, so they sailed up to security. Josh held his breath as he presented his fake passport and ID in the name of Josh Edwards. The navy didn't want him traveling under his own name for this assignment, and that order extended to any side trips.

Whoever had provided the fake documents excelled at his or her job, and Josh eased out a breath as he passed through security.

Thirty minutes later, juggling their coffee cups and carry-ons, they found seats in the small boarding area for Carib Air. It would take about ninety minutes to get to Isla Perdida.

Josh took a sip of coffee and scanned the other passengers over the lid. He pegged the couple in the corner of the waiting area, who couldn't keep their hands off each other, as newlyweds. The couple across from them must have a few more years of married life under their belts, as they paid more attention to their phones than each other.

Did marriage have to play out that way? He

slid a glance at Gina, on her own phone, texting her mother, no doubt. Had the flame died out between her and Ricky? Or had they been as passionate at the end as those two newlyweds? Maybe she never discussed him because she couldn't bear the pain of his loss.

She leaned toward him and whispered to him, her words tickling his ear. "I'll bet you anything those two over by the window are newlyweds."

"I was thinking the same thing." He rolled his eyes toward the preoccupied couple. "Probably married awhile longer."

A giggle bubbled from her lips and she covered her mouth. "Lots of single men, most likely businessmen checking on their assets."

Josh's gaze darted among the six men, all solo, all on laptops or some sort of device, all well dressed. His nerves jangled, and he took another sip of coffee. He'd been leery about a tail ever since he planned this trip. Any one of those guys could qualify.

He'd kept an eye out the back window of the taxi on the way to the airport but he hadn't noticed any cars following them—that didn't mean anything. Drug dealers, terrorists, spies all had ways of tracking people.

Another couple wandered into the boarding area, and Josh's muscles relaxed an inch more.

He didn't want to have to keep tabs on more than the six guys.

Gina chattered in his ear about the island. She told him again of her time there with her father, and once again his suspicions about her flared in his gut.

"It's beautiful but small." She swept her arm to encompass their fellow passengers. "As you can see, not a lot of young people go because there's very little nightlife, and not a whole lot of families go either since the attractions are mostly scenic—no zip lines, no swimming with dolphins, no catamaran cruises."

"A quiet getaway...or a place to fondle your money."

"You could say that."

Josh's gaze jumped back to one of the men. Had the man been watching them? He was accustomed to watching the nuances of a person's actions through a scope. It was harder to pick up on someone's movements from across a crowded room.

He asked Gina, "Are you done with your coffee?"

"I'm going to hang on to it and bring it with me on the plane."

"I'm going to visit that trash can next to the man in the red tie."

As he eased out of the seat, Gina exclaimed behind him. "Wait, what?"

Josh stretched and ambled toward the trash can, and the man sitting two seats from it. When he reached his destination, he lowered his eyelids and shifted his gaze to the man's body, below his neck. He didn't want to make eye contact.

Neat slacks and a tucked-in, striped button-down with one leather loafer resting on his knee made him fit right in with the other businessmen on the flight.

When Josh had approached the trash can, the man had stopped talking on his phone, and the device, encased in a leather holder with embossed gold letters in the corner, rested in his lap. Josh flipped the coffee cup into the can, brushed his hands together and turned away.

A quick glance at the man near the restrooms confirmed that he, too, had stopped talking on his phone.

Josh ducked next to Gina's chair. "I'm going to the men's room. Why don't you engage that nice couple in conversation while I'm gone?"

She nodded, her eyes wide but alight with comprehension.

As Josh walked toward the men's room and

the man stationed in front of it, he heard Gina say, "Is this your first trip to Isla Perdida?"

Josh passed the man near the restroom, his nose twitching at the guy's spicy cologne. Josh's gaze trailed to the cell phone the man clutched in one hand, and the blood thundered in his ears.

The man had the identical phone case as the man with the red tie. The embossed gold letters curled out from beneath the guy's fingers where they were wrapped around the case.

Josh stepped into the bathroom, but had no intention of sticking around in case the man outside decided to pay him a visit at the urinal. He joined another man at the sink and splashed cold water on his face.

Noticing the man's Miami Heat cap in the mirror, Josh nodded to him. "The Heat had a great season, huh?"

"Should've been longer."

Josh followed closely on the heels of the Heat fan out of the bathroom, brushing by the man with the leather cell phone case and giving half-hearted responses to the fan's enthusiastic analysis of the Heat's last playoff game. What did Josh know? He was a Knicks fan.

He parted ways with his newfound friend and took his seat next to Gina, who was still talking with the couple. He texted her.

The man with the red tie is talking to someone standing near the bathrooms with the exact same cell phone case. Don't look now.

When Gina's cell phone buzzed, she pulled it from her pocket and excused herself from the conversation with the couple.

She leaned into him, resting her head on his shoulder as she pretended to show him something on her phone. She said in hushed tones, with a smile on her face, "What does that mean?"

He pointed a finger at her display and laughed. "It means we're being followed. I'll wait to see who gets on the plane with us."

She tilted her face toward him, her smile wiped away. "How did that happen?"

"Not sure."

The loudspeaker interrupted their conversation with an announcement about boarding.

Josh grabbed his bag and pulled up Gina with him, and then positioned himself where he could keep an eye on both men. With the second boarding announcement, the two cell phone buddies got on their phones at the same time.

Oh, yeah. They were in cahoots.

The man with the red tie joined the end of the line. So, he was on his way to Isla Perdida. The man near the restrooms stayed at his post, making no move toward the boarding gate. Maybe he had been stationed there to try to take Josh out in the bathroom and give red tie unimpeded access to Gina.

Like he'd ever let that happen.

They shuffled toward the gate, and Gina pressed her shoulder against his arm. "Are we doing this?"

"Don't worry. I'll take care of him."

"I don't think the flight attendants are going to let you throw him off the plane."

"Wouldn't dream of it." As he handed his boarding pass to the attendant, he took one last look over his shoulder at the man by the bathrooms. At least he wouldn't be joining them on the island.

They shuffled onto the small plane with no seat assignments and Josh pinned his gaze on the empty seat behind the man, willing every other passenger away from it. Someone grabbed the seat before Josh could get to it, so he settled for a seat two rows behind the guy with the tie, allowing Gina to scoot in first and grab the window seat.

She raised her dark brows at him, but he just smiled.

The man with the red tie turned his head just once to see where they were sitting, and then settled into his seat, probably figuring his job was done until the plane landed.

Josh's job was just beginning.

Once everyone boarded and the flight attendant recited the safety instructions, the plane taxied and lifted off the runway. It cruised above Miami and out and over the deep blue sea.

Josh pulled his laptop case from beneath the seat in front of him and felt for the pen in the side pocket. He slid it out of the compartment and tucked it into the seat back in front of him.

When they reached cruising altitude, the flight attendants broke out the drink cart. As much as he could use a Bloody Mary right now, Josh ordered some orange juice.

Gina, still nursing her coffee from the terminal, passed on the drinks and ducked her head. "What are you going to do?"

"He may have gotten *on* the plane with us, but I'm going to make sure he doesn't get *off* the plane with us."

The plane bounced and Gina dug her fingers into her seat's armrest. "I guess since we're here and they're here, I can't claim ignorance anymore."

"They wouldn't have believed you anyway." He drained his juice and placed the empty plastic cup on Gina's tray table. Then he plucked the pen from the seat back and released his seat belt. "I'll be right back."

The bathroom was in the back of the airplane, but he'd have to improvise.

He staggered into the aisle and made his way toward the front of the plane...and the man in the red tie. The plane dipped again, and Josh grabbed someone's seat back.

Just as he drew level with the man's row, a flight attendant came up behind him. "Sir, are you looking for the lavatories?"

"Yes."

As soon as he answered, the man with the red tie whipped his head around, but Josh had anticipated his response.

In one fluid movement, Josh gripped the side of the man's seat, pressed the release for the needle embedded in his pen and jabbed it into the back of the man's neck.

The man bolted forward but before he could utter an exclamation, he slumped back into his seat and his head lolled to the side.

No point in sedating someone if the drug wasn't fast acting.

"The lavatory is in the back of the plane, sir."

"Thanks." Josh cupped the needle in his hand and backed up to let the flight attendant squeeze past him.

She didn't give a second look to the man sleeping in his seat like so many others.

Josh maneuvered to the back, weaving with

the turbulence common on these smaller planes. As he passed their row, Gina glanced up at him and he winked.

He locked himself in the bathroom and rolled back his shoulders. That was easier than he thought it would be…and badass.

He flushed the needle down the toilet, washed his hands and exited the lavatory, nodding at the woman waiting to use it. Then he slid into his seat and snapped on his seat belt.

"What happened? I didn't hear any commotion."

"I put our friend to sleep. He's not going to be getting off this plane for a long time."

Chapter Nine

As they exited the plane, Gina inched past the man in the suit and red tie as his seatmate nudged him.

"Sir? Sir, we've landed."

What would the flight attendants do when they couldn't wake him? Probably call an ambulance. Served him right.

She stared down into his face, but she didn't recognize him. Who were these strange people who had taken over Los Santos?

"Miss? Miss? This man is sleeping and won't move."

Gina exited the plane with Josh right behind her, propelling her forward with a hand at her back.

He said, "I doubt anyone saw me deliver the sleeping aid, but let's get out of here. He may be meeting someone else on this end."

Dragging her suitcase behind her, Gina quickened her pace to keep up with Josh's long legs. The humidity of the island had seeped into the terminal, and the light blouse she wore stuck to her back.

Josh's employers—whoever they were—had paid for the trip, or at least they would once they got the bill from Josh Edwards's credit card. Josh had assured her that money was no object, so he'd booked them into the most exclusive resort on the island—the same one she'd stayed at with her father on that fateful trip—the one that had changed her life.

Since they had no checked luggage, they sailed through Customs and snagged a taxi at the curb.

The driver placed their bags in his trunk and slid into the driver's seat.

Josh leaned forward and said, "Perdida Resort and Spa, *por favor.*"

The cabbie adjusted his rearview mirror. "First visit to the island?"

Josh answered for both of them, squeezing her knee while he did so. "Yes, first time."

"I have a cousin who can show you around the island. Good price just for you."

"Thanks, man, but we're doing more business than pleasure."

"Money, money, money." The driver grinned,

displaying his gold front tooth. "Isla Perdida has so much to offer but everyone sees the money."

Josh laughed. "We'll take some time to enjoy the resort if that makes you feel better."

"It does, senor. I'll give you my cousin's card just in case."

Thirty minutes later, the taxi pulled in front of the lush Perdida Resort and Spa. After he delivered their bags to the curb, the driver fished a card from his front pocket and extended it to Josh. "Just in case—for anything. They call him Fito, and he knows the island inside and out. Tell him his *primo* Robbie sent you."

"Gracias, Robbie." Josh pocketed the card and waved off the bellhops hovering to take their two small bags.

Gina's gaze swept the lobby. "Did you notice anyone suspicious?"

"Everyone looks suspicious to me now."

"Me, too." She pinched the ends of her blouse and fanned it up and down. "I could use a dip in the ocean."

Josh tapped a framed menu of spa services on the counter. "I could use a massage. My muscles are tied in knots right now."

"I guess navy SEALs aren't accustomed to the cloak-and-dagger stuff, huh?"

She drew her brows over her nose. What *were* SEALs accustomed to? She still didn't have a clue what Josh was doing at her father's compound. Protecting the CIA? Didn't seem like those CIA agents with the sniper rifles needed much protection. Maybe the SEALs had gotten the CIA in and out of the region.

She'd often wondered how the CIA had gotten into position around her father's compound. Must've had something to do with the SEALs. So, indirectly, Josh was responsible for her father's death—and Ricky's. And her father was indirectly responsible for his mother's death.

"Checking in?" The hotel clerk tapped the keyboard of her computer.

Josh slid their phony passports across the counter. "Josh and Gina Edwards."

Gina couldn't stop the butterflies that took off in her belly when she heard their names linked. They'd be sharing a room, pretending to be husband and wife.

Pretending was the key word. Behind closed doors they'd revert to…whatever it was they were. Partners? Coworkers? A couple linked by fate?

She watched his strong fingers grip the hotel's pen as he signed the registration form. Not that she'd mind continuing the pretense in their hotel room. Josh exuded strength and confidence— must be his military bearing. Josh didn't have a weak bone—or muscle—in his body.

After witnessing her father's machismo, Gina had convinced herself she wanted a softer man, but in Ricky's case softer didn't equal better.

"Take the elevator past the lobby restaurant to the sixth floor and let us know if there's anything we can do to make your stay more comfortable."

Gina had a fleeting thought. *Can you keep drug dealers off our tail while we're here?*

Josh swept the key cards from the counter and took Gina's arm. "Will do, thanks."

When they got to their room, Gina glanced at the king-size bed on her way to the sliding doors to the balcony. She stepped outside, and the moist island air caressed her cheek. She called back inside. "We have an amazing view—the pool below and the ocean beyond."

Josh followed her outside and braced his hands against the railing. "Wow. This sure beats any other place I'd be right now on deployment."

She pointed to the right. "Do you see that cluster of buildings over there? That's where the bank is."

"They know you as Gina De Santos, right?"

"Yes. My electronic thumbprint is on file. It's the only way we're getting into my father's safe-deposit box."

"I'd say that's secure."

"And that's why I'm confident anything my

father wanted to keep from his associates would be in that box."

"If the deal was going through, why would he keep it from his associates?"

"Maybe that's just it—the deal wasn't going through, or he wasn't sure or he didn't trust a bunch of terrorists. Imagine that?"

"That's kind of a case of the pot calling the kettle black, isn't it? Or are you going to try to tell me your father and husband were really honorable men."

Gina jerked away from him. Why did Josh always have to come back to that accusatory tone? He'd assured her that he didn't blame her for his mother's death at her father's orders. Was he lying to her? To himself?

She turned away from the beautiful view with ashes in her mouth. "I call dibs on the bed, but the sofa looks comfortable."

She slid the balcony door closed, leaving Josh out there by himself. Two could play that game. She was helping him, helping him and the US government, which had taken away everything she owned and had worked for in her life.

The money she'd used to start her restaurant hadn't come from her father. It had been an inheritance from her maternal grandmother, who'd been disgusted by her daughter's marriage to a drug dealer. Mami hadn't lived long enough to see her granddaughter make the same mistake—thank God.

The DEA hadn't cared about any of that. They'd seized everything after Ricky's death.

She dragged the zipper across her bag with such force, it broke. She cursed, which she never did around RJ. She cursed again.

The sliding door opened behind her. "Trying to keep the air-conditioning inside?"

"Yeah, that's it." She kept her back to him and pulled her toiletry bag from her suitcase. "We're too late to go to the bank today, so I'm going down to the beach to take that ocean swim."

"Closing at noon is really what I call banker's hours." He flicked the lock on the door. "I'll join you."

"We don't have to pretend to be married. You don't even have to pretend to like me." She stood up, clutching her skimpiest bikini to her chest. "I can handle a dip in the ocean by myself."

"I'm not going to allow you to run around Isla Perdida by yourself. They know we're here. I couldn't exactly murder the guy on the plane, so he may be showing up as early as tonight. Although the fact that we made him is going to make it hard for him to carry out his original assignment."

Josh unzipped his own suitcase and yanked

out a pair of board shorts. "And I don't have to pretend."

"What?" She scowled at him over her shoulder on the way to the bathroom.

"I don't have to pretend to like you. I like you…a lot."

She'd closed the bathroom door on his last two words. Had he meant for her to hear them? Probably just playing her like every other man in her life had done.

She leaned into the mirror, the red bikini clutched in her hands giving her face a rosy stain. She dropped the bathing suit to the floor.

Nope—that pink flush was totally due to Josh Elliott, damn him.

If he liked her a lot, why did he keep needling her about her father? Did he think she didn't know her father was a dirtbag? She knew better than anyone else.

Of course, she'd never told Josh that, but he had to know. Didn't he?

She stripped off her sticky clothes and kicked them into the corner. Then she shimmied into her bikini bottoms and clasped the top around her neck. She nabbed a plush towel from the shelf beneath the vanity and wrapped it around her body.

Exiting the bathroom, she stumbled to a stop

as she saw Josh tying the strings of his board shorts. "You changed out here?"

He spread his arms. "Is there a problem? I knew I'd be done before you."

She swallowed as she took in his hard muscles and washboard abs. *No problem at all.*

Her nose in the air, she dipped beside her suitcase and pulled out a beach cover-up. "Maybe you should just wait next time. I wouldn't appreciate surprising a naked man in my hotel room."

Liar.

Josh's mouth turned up on one side as he folded his clothes neatly, telling her that he totally knew she was lying.

Whistling, he brushed past her on the way to the bathroom, a plastic bag filled with men's toiletries tucked beneath one arm.

Was he flexing his muscles?

As soon as he disappeared into the cavernous bathroom, Gina whipped off the towel and pulled her black cover-up over her head. Just because he enjoying flaunting his assets, he couldn't expect her to feel the same way.

She was a mother, damn it.

The third curse word from her lips within the space of fifteen minutes gave her a reckless thrill, which she recognized all too well. She hadn't been this excited about being with a man since she'd first met Ricky, even though this man infuriated her most of the time.

Josh strolled back into the room, pointing at the towel she'd dropped on the bed. "I'm pretty sure the hotel will have beach towels by the pool and cold water and food. Maybe after we come in from the ocean, we should make a pit stop at the pool. The pool practically spills into the ocean."

"Sounds good. I'm getting hungry." Gina placed a hand on her stomach.

"I'll take my key and put it in my pocket." He held up his key card. "Everything else we can just charge to the room, so we don't have to leave anything on the sand when we go in the water."

"Actually, Isla Perdida has a low crime rate."

"That's because all the crime is the white-collar variety and taking place at the banks in town." Josh crouched next to his bag, rummaging through it.

"You have a point." A shiver ran through Gina as she remembered their purpose on the island. If they didn't find any clues in her father's safe-deposit box, would Josh suspect her of finagling a trip to Isla Perdida for her own reasons?

Why did she feel she had to make him trust her? He was here on some secret assignment and he had orders to protect her, whether or not he trusted her. But to have a man like Josh Elliott really and truly on her side? That would go a long way to restore her self-worth, which various government agencies had been tearing down since the assassinations last year.

Of course, Josh was one big, fat government representative, wasn't he? US Navy, CIA, FBI. Who knows what other acronym he supported?

Josh waved a bottle of sunscreen in the air. "We're both gonna need this."

"Bring it." She stuffed her feet into a pair of flip-flops. "I'm ready."

They made their way down to the lobby, which was open to the outdoors and the pool area. Gina waved to the honeymooning couple, who'd come over on their flight, now draped over a couple of chaise longues.

Her flip-flops smacked against the pool deck as she followed Josh to the private beach, for resort guests only.

As soon as Josh's toes touched the sand, three or four hotel employees swarmed them asking if they needed chairs, towels, a cabana, a drink.

It all sounded good to her, and Gina agreed to everything. If the US government was paying, they owed her anyway.

Josh straddled his chaise longue beneath the shade of a tent, inches away from the turquoise water lapping at the fine white sand. He squirted some sunscreen into his palm and smoothed it over his chest.

The glistening oil highlighted the flat planes of his pecs even more, and he resembled a photo in one of those hot navy SEAL calendars—not that she knew if those calendars even existed, but if they did, Josh could be April.

He finished rubbing his hands all over the front of his body, and then he tossed the bottle to her. "Can you get my back?"

Was he kidding?

She cleared her throat. "Sure."

He stood up and turned his back to her. "I already got my shoulders and my sides. If you could just hit my shoulder blades and below, that would get me covered."

She shook the bottle and squeezed out a puddle of white goop into her hand. She rubbed her hands together and dragged them down Josh's back, his warm, smooth flesh marred by a gnarly scar on his lower left side.

Her fingers trailed across the uneven ridges of skin. "What happened here?"

"Bullet wound."

She gasped, but pressed against the scar even harder. "I guess that's a hazard of the job."

"Happened before I was in the navy."

The words hung in the air as she waited for an explanation. None was forthcoming.

"Thanks." He spun around and zigzagged his index finger in the air, over her body. "I'll wait until you get oiled up."

"Oh, right." She still had on her black beach cover-up, which hit just above her knees. She dropped the sunscreen bottle onto her chaise longue and yanked the billowing garment up and over her head.

She immediately regretted packing her smallest bikini when she got a load of Josh's eyes, practically bugging out of his skull.

It was not like she was a skinny girl. She could fill out a bikini with the best of them, but why'd she have to choose this particular trip to do so?

She was a mother, damn it.

She grabbed the bottle and applied sunscreen over all the bits that had been covered up from the Florida sun these past several months.

After his initial gawking, Josh had appointed himself towel monitor, shaking out their two towels and placing them on the loungers.

Gina did her best to hit the spots within reach on her back, but if she didn't ask Josh for help she'd have red blotches all over her flip side from the intense Caribbean sun.

"Would you mind?" She held out the bottle.

"Same, I got my shoulders and sides, just need those hard-to-reach places covered."

"You got it."

She presented her back to him and nearly jumped out of her skin when his rough hands skimmed over her flesh.

He rubbed his hands in circles, rough enough so that her body kept swaying forward. She didn't object to his strategy for turning the application of sunscreen into an athletic event rather than a seductive one.

Then his fingertip tripped over the edge of her bikini bottoms, and heat that had nothing to do with the island surged through her body.

"That's good, thanks." She stayed turned around to compose herself and scoop her hair into a ponytail.

When she peeked over her shoulder at Josh, he'd returned to business by placing the sunscreen bottle on the table between them and straightening out his towel.

"Okay, ready for the water?"

"Absolutely." Gina took a few steps into the crystal clear ocean and continued stepping lightly until the water enveloped her waist-high. "Ah, perfect temperature."

Josh dashed past her, splashing and kicking up droplets of water, until he dived headfirst into a gentle wave.

A few snorkelers' tubes stuck up from the surface as they paddled with their fins on their search for sea life. A couple was swimming out to the reef that created a semicircle around their private beach, and a boat bobbed lazily just beyond the reef.

Josh's head popped up. "Feels great. It's not too deep and the waves are mild."

The water crept up to Gina's chest and she pushed her toes off the sandy bottom and dog-paddled toward Josh. If she were wearing a more practical bathing suit, she'd take a swim along that reef.

Josh ducked his head beneath the surface and came back up, sluicing his dark hair back from his face. "Maybe we should've picked up some snorkeling gear by the pool."

"We're not exactly on vacation." Gina tipped her head back and kicked out her legs so that she was floating on her back. Closing her eyes, she fluttered her hands at her sides to propel herself backward.

The sun warmed her cheeks and the salt water beaded on her body. The motion rocked her back and forth, and the tension in her muscles melted away. Why hadn't she taken a vacation since the raid at her father's compound? She'd needed one…badly.

After the deaths of her father and Ricky, she

never felt as if she deserved a vacation. The people who'd questioned and accused her had made her feel lower than dirt...even when she'd explained her situation to them.

That's why she hadn't told Josh anything about that time. She wouldn't be able to stomach the disbelief and contempt in his eyes.

She eased out a breath, the warm ocean water bubbling at her lips. As she blew out another breath, a pair of firm hands encircled her waist from below and she found herself airborne, flying over the surface of the water before landing several feet away with a splash.

Gurgling and sputtering, she flailed her arms to regain her balance and dug her toes into the sand to gain purchase. When she rubbed the water from her eyes, a view of Josh laughing materialized a few feet in front of her.

"That was not funny."

"Sure it was. You looked so peaceful, I couldn't resist."

"You're sadistic. I could've drowned or had a heart attack thinking you were a shark."

He snorted and started paddling toward her. "We're in about five feet of water with no rip current, and I'm pretty sure there are no sharks inside the reef."

"Really? You're pretty sure?" She tugged at

her bikini beneath the water to make sure everything was back in place.

He swam up next to her and put his hand vertically on his forehead to mimic a shark fin. "Well, I wasn't a shark, was I?"

"You'd better watch your back, SEAL."

He spit some water past her left ear. "Did you get your suit back on?"

"What does that mean?" She hit the surface of the water with her palm to splash water in his face. "Is that why you did it?"

He chuckled. "That's not why I did it, but it did turn out to be a side benefit."

What exactly had he seen? Those butterflies took flight in her belly again and a warm ache crept lower than that.

"You're...desperate."

"Honestly, that red bikini doesn't leave much to the imagination anyway."

"What are you talking about? It's just a bikini. It's a lot more modest than a couple of suits we passed on our way across the pool deck."

"Yeah, but those women... Let's just say they don't fill those suits out quite the way you do."

A tingling sensation raced all across her skin, and she crossed her arms. She had to gain control of this situation, of herself. "We're here under dangerous conditions with dangerous people after us on a dangerous mission."

Josh lifted his shoulders, water trickling down his bunched muscles. "Then it only makes sense that I'm with a dangerous woman with some seriously dangerous curves."

She didn't know how it happened. The water must've carried them closer together, but all of a sudden she and Josh were face-to-face, chest to chest even, as her breasts, safely back in their little triangles of red material, brushed the solid ridge of his pectoral muscles.

His hand rested on the curve of her hip, and the buoyancy of the water helped him to lift her up and draw her even closer.

Her toes bumped his shins and she could see droplets of water sparkling on the ends of his stubby black lashes. Her gaze dropped to his lips, parted and moist and she wanted nothing more than to taste the salt on his mouth.

His hand skimmed down her back and clutched one side of her buttocks to hold her in place as he angled his mouth over hers.

She sipped the salt water from his lips. Even his tongue tasted of the salty sea as he probed her mouth with it.

His fingers curled into the soft flesh of her bottom as he dragged her closer, his erection poking against her thigh.

She sucked his tongue harder and undulated her hips, so that his fingers slipped beneath the material of her bikini bottoms. The rough pads of his fingertips abraded her bare derriere, and she let out a breathy moan.

She could wrap her legs around him, right here in the ocean and let him take her. In fact, that's exactly what was going to happen. She hooked one leg around his hip, opening herself up to him.

He made a strangled noise as he broke their lip-lock and with one hand, reached under the water between them. He shoved aside the thin material of her bikini bottoms and swept one finger across her swollen flesh.

If he did that one more time, she'd come right here in the water, in view of…

"Hey, hey! Help!"

Josh jerked his head around and released her so abruptly, she sank before she started kicking her legs to tread water.

She looked over Josh's shoulder at the small motorboat beyond the reef and the man standing in it, waving his arms over his head.

"Looks like he's having trouble with his boat."

Gina launched forward in the water and swam toward the reef. As she turned her head to take a breath, Josh grabbed her ankle and she rolled onto her back. "What are you doing?"

"Take it slow. We don't know who this guy is."

"He's a tourist who needs help." She shook off his hand and backstroked closer to the reef and the sputtering boat. "You took care of the guy on the plane."

Josh pulled up beside her with a powerful stroke. "Let me go first. You wait here on the other side of the reef. Maybe he's just stuck and needs a lift from below, if his boat isn't damaged."

Gina allowed Josh to pass her but paddled after him. There was no way the man with the red tie's replacement was in Isla Perdida so soon and she found it hard to believe someone had already been here waiting for them, even though Josh had sounded that warning.

She squinted at Josh as he drew up to the reef and shouted something at the stranded tourist.

Two seconds later, Josh twisted his head around and yelled, "Duck! He's got a gun."

Chapter Ten

Josh dived beneath the surface, and a bullet whizzed by his head, slicing through the water. Through the clear Caribbean water, he could see Gina's legs kicking. Was she still upright?

He had a suspicion that a different fate awaited Gina once the phony tourist did away with him, but a bullet wound to her shoulder or arm would incapacitate her enough for the guy to scoop her up.

Josh snapped his legs hard in a breaststroke to reach Gina. He wrapped his arms around her legs and dragged her down.

With her eyes wide and bubbles spewing from her mouth, Gina joined him below and powered her arms through the water.

The man in the boat wouldn't be able to get his craft around the reef before Josh and Gina made it to shore, but he could climb onto the reef with his weapon to improve his aim. Somehow, Josh didn't think the man shooting at them would be bothered by the fact that disturbing sea life was a crime in Isla Perdida.

With his lungs ready to explode, Josh continued toward the beach, his arms and legs burning with the effort, Gina right beside him, matching him stroke for stroke, kick for kick.

She tugged on his board shorts and pointed toward the surface with her thumb.

He'd probably surprised her by dragging her under and she hadn't had time to take a deep breath. He wasn't going to allow her to surface on her own. Positioning himself between Gina and the man with the gun, Josh took her by the arms and rose through the water with her.

They broke the surface together and as he filled his lungs with air, Josh cranked his head over his shoulder. The boat that had feigned trouble had disappeared, and the small sailboat from earlier was now swaying behind the reef in its place. Had the sailboat scared off the shooter?

Josh wasn't taking any chances. He tapped Gina on the shoulder and she gave him a quick nod and ducked below again.

When the water became too shallow to completely cover them, Josh stopped swimming and stood up, planting his feet in the silky sand.

On her knees beside him, Gina coughed and sputtered.

"Are you okay?"

"I am now."

Josh swiveled his head from side to side, looking out for the motorboat, allowing Gina to gulp in some air and get her bearings. The few people in the shade of their cabana tents didn't even look up when he and Gina had staggered to the shore. Nobody had noticed the action in the water.

He swallowed as he glanced down at Gina, kneeling in the surf, her chest heaving, the water glistening on her skin. No wonder he hadn't been able to resist her out there in the sea. Couldn't stop himself from touching her, from kissing her, from wanting her.

And he'd put them both in danger because of it.

He crouched beside her and brushed a strand of wet hair from her cheek. "Do you need me to help you up?"

"I'm good." She coughed and allowed one more swell from the ocean to wash over her before pushing up to her feet with one hand, tugging at her bathing suit bottoms with the other.

The honeymoon couple strolled past them

hand in hand, and the woman waved. "How's the water?"

"Lovely." Gina smiled and murmured under her breath, "If you like bullets with your salt water."

Steps away in their cabana, Josh collapsed in his chaise longue. "I'm sorry. We should've never gone near that boat."

"Why are you apologizing?" Gina clutched her towel to her chest and dabbed her face with one corner. "I'm the one who insisted the guy was a hapless tourist who needed our help. I should've listened to you."

"I shouldn't be letting you insist anything. I'm supposed to be protecting you, and I never should've allowed you anywhere near that boat." He smacked his hand on the table between them, and knocked the bottle of sunscreen to the ground. "I was letting my other head rule."

Red flares claimed both of her cheeks. "What does that mean?"

"You know damned well what it means, Gina. I allowed my…lust for you to overrule my common sense."

She dropped to her chaise longue, wrapping the towel tightly around her body. "That's ridiculous. Even if we hadn't been…uh…kissing, that boat would've come at us anyway."

"Not if I'd been paying attention to our surroundings instead of how damned hot you looked in that little bikini."

"Should I have worn a one-piece suit up to my chin and down to my knees?" She tilted her head and squeezed water out of her ponytail.

"You shouldn't have been wearing anything at all."

"Really?" She raised one eyebrow. "I think that would've made things worse...or better depending on your perspective."

"You know what I meant. You should've never changed into a swimsuit, and we should've stayed in the room." He shook his head. "We were just tracked into the ocean somehow and someone's taking potshots at me and you're cracking jokes."

"Technically, that wasn't a joke and he was taking potshots at both of us."

"I wouldn't be too sure of that." Josh toweled off his head and when he emerged, Gina was staring at him. He asked, "What?"

"He was just shooting at you?"

"You tell me. I approached the reef, he turned a gun on me and I ducked. I saw the bullet plunge through the water. Did he shoot again? Did he shoot at you?"

"No." She nibbled on the end of one of her fingers. "He took another shot at you in the water, and then he stood there with his weapon raised waiting for you to surface."

"He wanted to take me out to get to you. Who knows? He may have had another weapon for you—one that shoots tranquilizer darts instead of bullets."

"You think so?" She hugged the towel more tightly around her body.

"They don't want you dead. They want to march you into that bank and have you give them access to your father's safe-deposit box, or whatever it is they think you're after on this island."

A waiter ducked his head beneath their awning. "Drinks, senor?"

"Sure, I'll have a cerveza, the island brand."

"Tequila sunrise for me—heavy on the tequila."

When the waiter left, Josh raised his brows. "Still need to take the edge off, huh?"

"Look at this." She held out one trembling hand. "I can't believe how stupid I was to trust a stranger like that."

"I can't believe how distracted I was to let you." He put on his sunglasses and reclined his lounger. "That can't happen again, Gina, and I apologize."

She smacked his calf. "You have nothing to apologize for. Sun, surf, skin—we just got carried away. This island could put a spell on you if you let it, and we've been under a lot of pressure."

"Back to business then. The bank opens at nine o'clock tomorrow morning. Make sure you bring everything you need to prove your identity and leave the fake ID at the hotel."

"I've been through the routine before with my father. I know what to do."

"Can I ask you a question?" He crossed his right index finger over his left in a protective gesture because every time he asked her anything about her father or his business, she got defensive.

"Yes."

"What were you doing here with your father, and why did he take you to the bank?"

She blew out a breath and shoved her sunglasses up to her head. "He wanted to prove a point to me."

"Which was?"

"You have to promise me you won't relay this information to anyone you work for—not the CIA, not the DEA."

"Is it going to get anyone killed?"

"No."

He held up two fingers. "Scout's honor, even though I was never a Boy Scout."

"Didn't think so." She chugged some water

from one of the bottles the waiter had placed on the table while taking their order. "He wanted to show me where my mother's money was coming from."

"Why? You didn't know?"

"No. My father's family in Colombia had money. Mom had always told me that the settlement she received from my father for the separation had come from his family's money."

"That didn't turn out to be true." Josh had scooted forward on the chaise longue, digging his feet into the sand on either side of it.

When the waiter appeared with their drinks, Josh almost tossed him out for interrupting the flow of Gina's thoughts. She'd never told him this much before. Maybe kissing her in the ocean *hadn't* been such a mistake—his body hadn't thought so at all.

He thanked the waiter and scribbled the room number and his signature on the check. Wrapping his fingers around the beer bottle, Josh turned to Gina and waited.

She put her lips to the straw stuck in her glass and took a sip of the orange concoction inside. Then she bit off the point of the pineapple slice that was balanced precariously on the edge of her glass.

Josh held his breath.

She licked her fingers and then wiped them

off on the towel still encasing her body like armor. "My father's family shunned him and disinherited him when they learned he was a drug dealer. He and my mother didn't get a dime from them."

"Why did your father want to show you where your mom was getting the money?"

"To control me."

Josh finally took a sip of his own drink. "Why did he need to control you?"

She pinned him with her dark eyes, flashing fire. "Why do you think? By this time, I'd figured out what he did for a living, and I wanted nothing to do with him. I wanted to walk away from it all, from him…from my marriage."

Josh's pulse jumped. *Her marriage.* Had she wanted to leave Ricky? It's what he'd wanted to hear from her all along. "Did your father think you'd rat him out?"

"I don't think so." She shrugged. "I probably wouldn't have gone that far. I didn't know anything the DEA hadn't already figured out."

"Your father didn't realize that?"

"My father was a man who took very few chances…even with his daughter."

"So, he showed you the money, and maybe how it was laundered for your mother, to prove your mother's complicity in his crimes. If you ever told anyone about the money or any of his business deals—" Josh drew a finger across his throat "—he'd either cut off your mother or she'd go down with him—at least for the financial crimes."

"That's it. My father knew I'd never do anything to disrupt my mother's life."

"Why didn't he let you walk away after that? He'd just assured your silence. Why were you still visiting him at his compound at the end?"

She sighed and sucked down half of her drink. "It's so complicated—*familia*."

Josh's heart sank. "You mean no matter what your father, your mother or your...husband did, you could forgive and forget to keep it in the family?"

Gina snorted and tossed back the rest of her drink. "No. It was my father who had a warped sense of family loyalty and what that means.

"I wasn't at his compound that day or any other day to find comfort in the bosom of my family."

"What then?" Josh pressed his cold, sweating bottle against his forehead.

"My father wanted—no, demanded—to see RJ."

"That's what he wanted from you? That's why he wanted to keep you close?"

"RJ is his only grandchild. He was afraid I'd take him away and he'd never see him again."

"Would you have done that?"

She blinked. "In a second."

"Your father threatened to take your mother's money away from her or turn her in if you didn't bring RJ around?"

"It was worse than that, Josh." She dropped her chin to her chest and shook her glass so that the ice tinkled.

"Worse?" Josh licked his dry lips and switched his beer for a bottle of water. Since Gina had turned toward a confessional mood, he wanted to find out the truth behind her marriage to Ricky Rojas.

He had to know how Gina felt about the man he'd killed.

"What was your husband's take on all this? He was okay with your son being in the company of a drug kingpin?"

She flicked her wet ponytail over her shoulder. "Ricky did whatever my father told him to do. In fact, he married me to get in with my father."

Josh could think of a million reasons why a man would want to marry Gina, but getting in good with her father wasn't one of them.

"Ricky knew all about Hector De Santos and Los Santos when you two started dating?"

"Ricky knew about my father *before* we started dating. He knew about my father before

I did." She rolled the slender glass between her palms. "Ricky targeted me. He managed to get a job in the same restaurant where I worked and then really laid it on thick. I was such an idiot."

"Why would you even suspect Ricky's motives?" Josh shifted forward, walking his feet in the sand, and grabbed one of her hands, chilly and wet from the glass. "I'm sure a smooth SOB like Ricky knew just what the ladies wanted to hear."

"He knew what *this* lady wanted to hear." She jabbed a thumb at the towel still covering her chest. "I remember my father from when I was a child—the fights with Mom, the violence, the swaggering machismo. I wanted none of it, and Ricky played into that. He was a poet, a musician...an aspiring crook."

"How long into your marriage before he made the move toward your father?"

"Long enough for me to be pregnant with RJ. Ricky knew that would be the glue, the true way into my father's heart—and his cartel."

"So, that's what you meant by worse. You were all tied up with your father, your husband, your child. I'm sure you had your reasons to stay." Josh released her hand and skimmed a palm across the top of his head.

He understood her apprehension about taking RJ and leaving, but the words from her mouth still sounded like excuses to him—just like the excuses his mother used to make.

"That is *not* what I meant." Gina put her glass down on the table with a click. "You think I stayed with my husband and brought my precious son to visit my murdering, psychotic father because of family ties and some money of my mother's?"

She sloughed off her towel and straddled the chaise longue, her shoulders back and her spine straight. "I brought my son around because my father threatened to take RJ and keep him away from me forever, bringing him into the business."

Chapter Eleven

Through the shade of her sunglasses, Gina watched the emotions play across Josh's face. Did she see relief in there somewhere?

Would her story finally convince him that she'd wanted no part of her father's drug empire and no part of her marriage with Ricky?

When Josh spoke, his words came out in measured, dull syllables as if he were suppressing a great rage. "How did your father intend to keep your son from you?"

"Really?" She shook her glass of rapidly melting ice. "My father had money and power in Colombia—politicians, judges, law enforcement officials—all in the palm of his hand. He gave me a taste of that power once, took RJ right away from me for a week."

"Your husband was okay with it?"

"My husband aided and abetted my father, and was handsomely rewarded for doing so.

Even if I had initiated divorce proceedings against Ricky, my father would've seen to it that Ricky would win sole custody of RJ and I would've been shut out completely." Gina shivered in the heat.

A muscle ticked in Josh's tight jaw. "Is that why you were so anxious to find out if Ricky was alive?"

"Did you think I was anxious to reunite with my dead husband to rekindle our great romance?" Her lip curled. Ricky the poet and musician had completely morphed into something unrecognizable once he'd wormed his way into her father's organization. She never let him touch her again.

"I'm sorry. I shouldn't have made any assumptions."

The waiter showed up at their cabana again and while Josh waved him off, Gina held up her glass. *"Uno más, por favor."*

Josh wasn't finished with her yet. "Did you tell the DEA about your father's threats?"

"Yeah, but I don't think they believed me, and of course I didn't say anything about my mother's money or this bank account."

"Maybe that's why the agents didn't believe your story. They sensed you were lying about something."

"They were right." She collapsed back in the

chaise longue, a great weight sloughing off her shoulders. "Do you trust me now?"

"Trust you? It was never about trust, Gina."

"Oh, yeah, it was. Sometimes you looked at me like..." She scrunched up her nose. "Like I was a bug to be squashed, and that was even before you found out about your mother."

His eyebrows jumped to his hairline. "I never thought of you as a bug—to be squashed or otherwise."

She waved her hands. "Okay, well, maybe we can just put that behind us. I wasn't in league with my father or my husband or any of Los Santos. I was just trying to protect my mother, my son. Now I'm trying to help you."

"I'm supposed to be helping you."

"Can't we help each other? You seem like a guy who needs help."

The waiter ducked beneath their awning with another tequila sunrise on a tray. Josh signed for the drink.

Toying with the swizzle stick loaded with fruit, Gina took a sip of the sweet drink but had lost her desire for it once her confession had ended.

"This—" Josh spread his hands "—isn't personal for me, you know. I was sent here on assignment by my superiors, and I obey orders."

"Hmm." She dragged her sunglasses to the

tip of her nose with one finger and studied him over the top of the frame. "Not personal, huh?"

"You mean what happened in the water between us? That was... What did you say? Sun, surf and skin? You're a damned attractive woman, Gina, sexy as hell. I'm a red-blooded, American male, and I made a mistake."

She flicked her fingers at him. "I'm not talking about the...heat between us. There's something about this assignment that has gotten under your skin. Taking down Los Santos and making sure they stay out of business—" she thumped her chest with her fist "—means something to you, now more than ever."

He lifted his broad shoulders. "Law, order, truth, justice and the American way."

"If you say so, SEAL." She sucked down some more tequila.

"Are you ready to pack it up?" He leveled a finger at her half-full glass. "Or are you going to finish that?"

"They're pretty strong. That first one did the trick, took the edge off after our mad swim to shore." She dipped her head and scanned the ocean. She could just make out two heads bobbing close to the reef—*must be the honeymoon couple*. "Where do you think he went?"

"Back where he came from. My guess is that he lives here. Could just be a gun for hire, or maybe he's on retainer with the cartels to take care of business. There's no way Los Santos got someone to this island before we even arrived."

"Is it just Los Santos I have to worry about?" She stood up and pulled her beach cover-up over her head. "There were two parties screwed in that deal, right? If there are missing weapons as well as drugs, the people on the receiving end of those weapons must be just as invested in finding them as Los Santos is in finding the drugs."

"That's true."

She wedged a hand on her hip. "So, what are we talking about here, SEAL? Terrorists? Are you telling me I have a terrorist cell on my tail?"

He picked up her drink and downed it. "Yeah, you do. *We* do."

WHEN THEY GOT back to the hotel, Josh decided to pay a visit to the harbor to inquire about boat rentals and to see if he could get a line on anyone who'd rented a small motorboat that afternoon.

He paused at the hotel door. "You're not planning to take any more swims in the sea, are you?"

"Nope. I'm going to take a shower and sit on the balcony with my book, feet up."

"Good. Don't leave the room and don't open

the door. Don't order room service or anything from housekeeping and keep the chain on."

"You're making me nervous." In fact, she'd been more than nervous once Josh admitted what she'd suspected deep down all along— she had some very bad guys after her.

"That's not a bad thing, to be nervous." He smacked the doorjamb. "I'll be waiting outside until I hear you lock and chain the door."

She turned from the window and crossed the room. "I'm on it."

Stepping into the hallway, Josh pulled the door closed behind him and Gina locked the top bolt and hooked the chain across.

She shut and locked the balcony doors for good measure, even though their room sat on the sixth floor, the top floor of the hotel. Then she grabbed her toiletry bag and headed for the bathroom.

She dropped her cover-up on the floor. She peeled off her bikini and stuck it in one of the sinks, running cool water over it. What had possessed her to pack that suit? She had a one-piece that covered a heckuva lot more, but what fun would that have been?

"Face it, girl." She braced her hands against the vanity and leaned in for a close look at her flushed face. "You wanted that SEAL before you even knew he was a SEAL."

She couldn't even explain her immediate chemistry with Josh to herself. Of course, he had the dark good looks she loved in a man and a body that wouldn't quit for days, but there had been some connection between them from the get-go.

Maybe it had to do with the fact that he was there in Colombia when her life had changed forever. What he was doing there, she still wasn't quite sure. It was all kind of strange and mysterious.

She yanked back the semicircular curtain on the shower and walked into the huge, tiled space that sported two showerheads. Perfect for showering with someone, but Josh had made it clear that what had happened in the ocean between them wouldn't happen again.

Sighing, she cranked on both faucets just because she could, allowing the dual jets to spray her front and back at the same time. Decadence.

She finished showering and put on a sundress—loose, modest, comfortable. She grabbed a book and padded out to the balcony with bare feet. Hanging over the railing, she watched the people at the pool, spotting the older couple from the plane but not the newlyweds. They were probably making out in one of the cabanas—lucky.

She sat in one of the chairs, her face shaded and her legs stretched out into the sunshine. Closing her eyes, she wiggled her toes.

She'd been confident her father had left something in his safe-deposit box relating to this deal, but what if she were mistaken? That's another reason why she'd told Josh about her past and the way her father had controlled her. If they found nothing in the safe-deposit box, Josh wouldn't suspect her of ulterior motives in suggesting the trip to Isla Perdida.

After seeing the swimsuit she'd packed, he might suspect her of other ulterior motives—and he wouldn't be far from the mark. The guy had it all in the looks department, but he was no pretty boy. His broad shoulders looked like they could carry the worries of the world...or at least her worries. Even the scars on his body were sexy because she knew he'd gotten them in the commission of good and not evil. Although there was the scar from the bullet wound he'd claimed he'd gotten pre–active duty days. He'd probably gotten it jumping in front of someone else.

A loud knock at the door made her start, and she scrambled out of her comfortable seat and rushed across the room. She peered through the peephole at the man of her recent daydreams.

She unchained the door and opened it. "Any luck?"

"A little." He squeezed past her and turned, holding a gun by the barrel.

Covering her mouth with one hand, she asked, "Where did you get that?"

"Remember Robbie, our taxi driver? He mentioned his cousin?"

"You got a gun from our taxi driver's cousin?"

"Robbie mentioned he could get anything for us."

"So, you naturally assumed that meant a weapon?"

"I read between the lines. His cousin is a go-to guy on the island—drugs, women, weapons. After today's…excitement in the water, I figured I'd need a piece for tomorrow's visit to the bank."

"The bank has metal detectors. You won't get in with that."

"I will if I'm your bodyguard. I already checked with Fito."

"Fito is Robbie's cousin?"

"Yep."

"I feel so—" she spun around with her arms outstretched "—useless. All I managed to do was take a shower and sit on the balcony, enjoying the view."

"That's all you needed to do." Josh crouched in front of the hotel safe in the closet and stashed the gun inside. "I'm going to get cleaned up, and we'll have some dinner."

"You didn't find out anything at the harbor about someone renting a boat?"

"No, but my new best friend, Fito, might be able to help me out there, too."

"If this guy's so darned helpful, maybe he helped the other guy get the boat and the weapon he used to shoot at us." She chewed her bottom lip. "Can you trust him?"

"I can trust him as much as the next payoff. I have no illusions about him, but I'm going to use him when I can." Josh closed the closet door and brushed his hands together. "I'm going to take a shower. You can return to the balcony and continue doing what you were doing out there."

Thinking about Josh Elliott.

"You'll like that shower." She slid open the door to the balcony and closed it behind her. She didn't need to hear that water running and imagine Josh's perfect form getting wet under two sprays of water.

She hung over the side of the balcony and spotted the honeymoon couple by the side of the pool, sitting across from each other at a table, not even talking. Were they sick of each other already?

She shifted her gaze from the pool to the sea beyond. She remembered those heady newlywed days. She'd been so young…and stupid. Ricky had been insistent upon starting a family immediately. She'd been touched by his enthusiasm until she realized the baby was a way to cement her to him and cement him to her father.

She didn't regret one day of RJ's sweet life, so she had a hard time looking back and wishing things had been different. Everything had changed anyway when the CIA decided to assassinate the leading members of Los Santos once they'd gotten in bed with a terrorist cell. That action had probably saved her life…and RJ's.

The door slid open behind her, and Josh put his hands on her shoulders. "Doing okay? How's the view?"

No regrets at all.

She inhaled his fresh scent and straightened up. "I'm fine, and the view is beautiful, as long as it doesn't contain any boats bearing men with guns."

"Pool area still crowded?"

"Plenty of people down there, including our honeymooners from the plane even though they seem to have gotten a little tired of each other."

She turned, and Josh dropped his hands from her shoulders. "Where are we having dinner? I'm starving."

"I know there are plenty of five star restaurants on this little island, but would you mind if we just ate in the hotel restaurant? I'd prefer we keep a low profile here."

"I don't think the hotel's restaurant is too shabby either, so that's fine with me." She gave him the once-over in his cargo shorts and light blue button-down shirt.

He tugged on the hem of his shirt. "Too casual?"

"I'm sure it's fine. Most people at the hotel seem to wander from the beach to the pool to the restaurant without breaking their stride."

"Then I'm ready."

"Just need my shoes." She walked back into the room and slipped on a pair of sandals while Josh locked the doors to the balcony.

By the time they got down to the restaurant, people were crowding the edge of the pool area to watch the sunset and had already nabbed all the tables in the dining area.

Josh scanned the packed restaurant. "Should've figured this would be a popular time to eat. We can come back later or maybe order room service."

"I can't wait." Gina patted her stomach.

A woman popped up at one of the prime tables, outside on the patio and facing the sea, and waved. "Over here."

"It's the couple from the plane. I don't think they ever went up to their room."

"Maybe because they already knew what a madhouse it was here at sunset." Josh touched her elbow. "Should we go over?"

A hostess dressed in a flowing pareu floated toward them. "Excuse me. The couple at the edge of the patio would like you to join them for dinner. We are fully booked, otherwise."

Gina shrugged. "Why not? We can eat and run if they bore us."

Josh turned to the hostess. "Yes, we'll join them, thank you."

The hostess guided them to the best seats in the house, and Gina and Josh greeted their new-found friends.

Gina introduced Josh to Tara and Roger, as they'd exchanged names at the airport.

Tara smiled and squeezed her husband's arm. "We were warned about getting in early to watch the sunset."

Gina smiled. "Thank you so much. I was about ready to faint from hunger."

"I can imagine, since you had quite a swim in the ocean today."

Josh nudged Gina's toe with his foot. As if he had to warn her.

Nodding, Gina said, "Yeah, it was, uh, invigorating."

"I'm glad I'm not the only one going casual." Josh tipped his head at Roger, still dressed in his board shorts, although he'd topped them with a green polo shirt.

"We didn't want to miss out on getting a table. Lucky for you we didn't go back to our room or wander around the waterfront."

Josh kicked her under the table, and Gina slid a quick sidelong look at him. Did he think she was going to tell Roger about the taxi driver's cousin and the gun?

"Yep, lucky for us. Thanks again for asking us to join you. Have you ordered yet?"

"Just drinks." Tara picked up the menu. "But the waiter told us about the specials."

A waiter arrived with a tray bearing two margaritas.

"Those look good. I think we'll have a couple of those."

"That tequila sunrise I had on the beach was pretty good."

Josh kicked her again and chuckled. "But now it's sunset. In fact, we'll have a pitcher, please."

If he didn't stop kicking her, he'd get a glass

of water in his face. Why was he so set on margaritas and an entire pitcher of them?

They exchanged more small talk about the island until the waiter returned with two more glasses and a pitcher of icy margaritas. The waiter poured drinks for Gina and Josh, and then took their orders.

After another fifteen minutes of chitchat, Josh grabbed the handle of the pitcher and held it up. "Top those off for you?"

Before Tara or Roger could answer, Josh was tipping the pitcher over their glasses, filling them to the top. "We've had a stressful day. I need this right now."

Josh wrapped a hand around his glass and gestured in the air as half his drink sloshed over his hand. *"Salud."*

Now it was her turn to kick him under the table. Why was he telling good old Tara and Roger about their stressful day? Did he *want* them to start prying?

Tara eyed him over the wide rim of her glass. "I thought Isla Perdida was paradise? You mean you actually experienced stress here?"

Josh sputtered and clamped a napkin to his mouth. "Gina told you we were combining a little business with our pleasure? Well, it's the business part that's stressing us out."

"We wouldn't know about that, would we,

Tara? It's strictly pleasure for us." Roger kissed his wife's hand.

"Then drink up."

Gina had no idea what game Josh was playing, but he ordered another pitcher and poured another round of drinks for everyone. Tara and Roger seemed reluctant to imbibe any more, but didn't want to offend Josh so they kept sipping away.

She didn't blame the honeymooners. She'd tossed the contents of at least one glass into the bushes to her left, but pretended to be drinking along with the rest of them.

The food arrived and Josh continued to get louder and louder. He liberally sampled food from the other couple's plates and ordered a third pitcher of margaritas.

Tara had indicated that they were from New York and without ever revealing his own connection to the state, Josh asked Roger questions about it as if he were planning on taking a vacation there.

Gina giggled along with his antics, while casting apologetic looks toward Tara. Roger didn't seem to mind at all. While Tara's heavy lids drooped over her eyes, Roger's speech began to slur and he had trouble retrieving his napkin from the ground.

"I have an idea." Josh snapped his fingers for

the waiter. "Let's hit one of those cabanas on the beach and finish the night with a few cocktails in the sand."

Tara waved her napkin as if waving a white flag. "I'm really tired."

Roger shot his new wife a very unnewlywed glance. "We'd be happy to, mate."

Josh scribbled on the check. "This one's on us."

"Very generous of you." Roger had to help his wife out of her chair.

Josh stumbled for good measure, but Gina didn't think for one minute he was drunk. She grabbed his arm and the four of them tripped out to the sand.

Josh kept prodding them on to the last cabana on the beach, even though it seemed as if Tara and now Roger could barely lift their feet from the sand to take their next step.

When they reached the tent, Josh helped Roger into a chaise longue and then poured Tara into hers. Within minutes, the two newlyweds were passed out cold.

Gina turned on Josh and, in a harsh whisper, asked, "Why in the world did you get those two drunk, and what are the odds that they'd both pass out?"

"Shh." Josh crouched beside Roger and transferred some items from the comatose man's pockets to his pockets. Then he plunged his hand in Tara's purse.

"What are you doing, robbing them?"

Josh held up a key card. "Let's hurry. We'll have a couple of hours to search their room."

"S-search their room?" Her eyes widened as her gaze shifted from one passed-out person to the other.

"What did you think was going on in the restaurant, Gina? These two are the enemy."

Chapter Twelve

Gina's feet felt rooted in the sand, and her jaw dropped open. The handsy newlywed couple, the enemy?

"What did you do to them?"

"Slipped a little something in their margaritas."

"You're a regular walking pharmaceutical repository. People are just dropping in your wake."

Completely sober, he took her arm. "I'll explain on the way to their room. Tara conveniently left her key card in the little envelope with their room number. She's no pro."

When they reached the hotel, Josh took her hand and they skirted the restaurant. No sense in having anyone wonder where the other drunken couple went.

As they raced through the lobby and into the elevator, Gina asked, "How did you know?"

"Tara let it slip that they were from New York. When she did, Roger shot her a look that could kill. Seemed odd, so I brought up something about New York later and it was clear they'd never lived there. Something you said earlier struck me as odd, too. A honeymooning couple that stays at the pool all day, and then the beach and then back at the pool where you said they hardly spoke to each other, let alone kissed?

"Wouldn't a honeymoon couple who were all over each other like these two were want to spend more time in their hotel room than at the pool? And why were they going down to the water just after we'd been ambushed? To see that the job had been done on me and to help out with you?"

Gina shivered and hunched her shoulders. "But they seemed so…normal."

"And did you catch the *mate* business from Roger when the drug started taking effect on him? No New Yorker I know uses *mate*."

"Do you think they were working with the red tie man on our flight?"

"I don't know, Gina." He squeezed her waist.

Her blood ran cold, and she tripped to a stop as they exited the elevator. "You think both groups are here, don't you? Los Santos and the terrorist organization. They're both after us at the same time."

"Could be." He rubbed a circle on her back. "C'mon, we're almost there."

She scooped in a deep breath and hooked two fingers in the belt loop of Josh's shorts. They didn't see anyone else in the hallway.

When they reached the room, Josh slid the key home and held out a hand to keep her back. "Hang on. We don't know what we're going to find in here."

She hung back in the hallway until he waved her inside. The faux newlyweds' room was much like their own with one interesting detail—two beds.

Josh pointed at the beds. "An odd sleeping arrangement for a couple of honeymooners, wouldn't you say?"

Gina nodded. Either Tara and Roger weren't as committed to their deception as she and Josh were…or they weren't as attracted to each other.

"I'm going to search their suitcases. You look through the closets, drawers and bathroom."

Gina tiptoed to the closet even though she knew Tara and Roger were out cold on the beach with little chance that anyone would discover them until morning, unless they came to in the few hours that Josh gave them. She slid back the door and ran her hand along a few shirts and blouses neatly arrayed on hangers. Careful not to disturb any shoes, she crouched and inspected the floor of the closet.

"Their safe is locked."

"Don't worry. I have a surefire way of getting in there."

"That does not make me feel very confident about hotel safes." She stood on her tiptoes, her gaze sweeping across the iron and a few extra pillows on the closet shelf. "I don't see anything in the closet."

Josh came up behind her. "I found a few interesting items."

She glanced down at his hands, cupping an assortment of bottles and vials. "Looks like you're about to add some inventory to your pharmacy."

"Matches the pills I took from Roger's pocket." He shook one of the bottles. "If I hadn't drugged them first, it would be us passed out on the beach…or worse."

"That's probably why they were so eager to go with us. They hadn't figured out that we—you were onto them and they planned to slip something in our drinks on the sand."

"Exactly. Of course, they weren't thinking very clearly by that time." Josh knelt in front of the safe and after many beeps and clicks, the door swung open. He reached inside the small space and pulled out a couple of passports.

Gina leaned over his shoulder as he flipped them open and read from the passport page. "Roger Nealy and Tara Nealy. Are those fake?"

"As fake as ours." He replaced them in the safe, closing the door but not locking it.

"Shouldn't you lock it up again?"

"I would if I knew how to reset it with the code they used—I don't."

"They're going to figure out we got the jump on them."

"That's okay. They won't pretend to come at us like the hapless honeymooners anymore. The more of them we expose, the less likely they'll be able to surprise us."

Crossing her arms, she said, "Good. I don't like surprises."

Josh's height allowed him to get a better look at the closet shelf, and he lifted the pillows and checked out the iron.

"The iron isn't some kind of secret weapon?"

"I have no idea. I'm a sniper not a spy."

She tilted her head and scrunched up her face. "You…"

"Bathroom? Did you check it out yet? We need to get a move on."

"No."

Chewing her bottom lip, she trailed after him

as he strode to the cavernous bathroom, sporting the same dual-head shower as theirs.

"Check her bag." He tipped his head toward a toiletry bag hanging on a hook as he pawed through a masculine version on the counter.

"Do you think they have any weapons in the room?" If Gina hoped to find any poison or hypodermic needles among Tara's stuff, the department store makeup and cleansers were a disappointment. At least this particular spy was thrifty.

"They weren't carrying any, and we know they couldn't have brought them on the plane. Maybe their cohort, the guy on the boat provided them with some guns.

"Tara has nothing."

"Roger either. Nothing in their suitcases with contact info either."

"You didn't expect to find a to-do list, did you? Number one, incapacitate the SEAL. Number two, kidnap the drug kingpin's daughter."

He tugged on a lock of her hair. "Not quite like that."

A cell phone buzzed and Gina patted the pocket of her purse. "Not mine."

"Not mine either." Josh dipped his hand into his shorts pocket and withdrew a vibrating cell phone. "It's Roger's."

"You got Roger's phone?"

"Lifted it from his pocket." He held the phone in front of his face. "Even better. This is a text message, not a phone call."

"You're not going to…?"

"Pretend I'm Roger?" He skimmed his finger across the phone's display. "Watch me."

"What does it say?" She squinted at the words on the display.

Josh read them aloud. "'What's going on?'"

"Good question. What are you going to respond?"

"I'm going to give this texter the good news. My lovely bride and I have the couple in question passed out in a couple of lounge chairs on the beach."

"You're going to send him right to Tara and Roger?"

"I'm going to send him right to me."

Gina grabbed his wrist. "What does that mean?"

"I'm going to direct this guy to the cabana, and I'm going to lie in wait and get some answers."

"That's…dangerous." She tried to swallow but her dry throat made her gag.

"Don't forget. I have that little piece from Fito."

"Josh, you can't shoot someone on Isla Perdida. You can't leave a dead body on the beach."

"Who said anything about any dead bodies? Tara and Roger will still be conked out. This man won't be expecting me, so I'll have the element of surprise. I'll get him at gunpoint and start asking a few questions. I'll be okay."

He twisted his arm out of her grasp and started tapping the phone's screen. "There. Forty-five minutes should give me enough time to retrieve that gun and conceal myself in the cabana with the newlyweds."

"Me, too."

"No way."

"I'm going with you, Josh."

"You're going to stay in the room with the door locked. I don't want you anywhere near this man or this situation."

"You just said it wasn't going to be dangerous."

"I didn't say that." He cupped her face with one hand. "Let me face the danger. You've faced enough—all your life."

Her nose tingled and she blinked her eyes to dispel the tears gathering there. Nobody, not her mother, not Ricky, not the DEA, CIA or the FBI had ever once acknowledged the fear and danger she'd lived with since finding out about her father.

She thought it had come to an end that day at her father's compound, but she couldn't have been more wrong. Only now she had Josh Elliott to protect her and if he thought she needed to stay in the room for this encounter, she'd do it.

She nodded and sniffed. "All right. I'll wait in the room, but you'd better be careful."

"This is what I do."

Was it? Then what had he been doing at her father's compound?

THEY MADE THEIR way back to their room and Josh had to stuff his hands in his pockets so he wouldn't be tempted to put them all over Gina. He'd expected her to put up more of a fight about being left behind, but she showed a lot of common sense and restraint.

She must've realized that her presence would've added nothing to the trap. She didn't have a weapon of her own, not that he wouldn't have trusted her with one, and he didn't need for her to cause a distraction or have his back. He just needed to know she was safe in the room.

He closed and locked their hotel room door behind them and dived for the safe in the closet. Cradling the gun, he sat on the edge of the bed next to her and loaded it.

"Can I see it?"

Josh extended the butt of the gun to her and she gripped it, testing its heft and weight. "Nice little piece."

"Not bad."

"Please be careful. I shudder to think what the Isla Perdida *policía* would do to you if they arrested you for murder."

"That's not going to happen." He leaned forward and kissed the top of her head. Then he took the gun from her and stuck it in the waistband of his shorts.

She wiggled her fingers in the air. "Shouldn't you change clothes? Black? Camouflage?"

"And stick out like a sore thumb in this resort? This will work." He pushed up from the bed and stood by the door, his fingers on the door handle. "Remember, stay in this room and don't open the door for anyone. I'll be back before you know it and hopefully somewhat wiser about who's here and why."

As he turned toward the door, Gina jumped from the bed and threw her arms around his neck. She planted a hard kiss on his mouth.

"Come back in one piece. I can't do this, any of this, without you."

On his way to the elevator, Josh brushed his fingers across his tingling lips. Gina had found a surefire way to get him to come back in one piece…as long as he could get the jump on this guy.

Once again, he made a wide berth around the pool deck and restaurant on his way to the beach. The resort had strung mini LED lights along the path to the beach and had stationed electric torches every few feet along the sand.

Josh kept clear of all the lights and hung back in the shadows as he ducked behind each cabana he passed until he reached the last one. He dropped to his hands and knees and lifted the edge of the tent where it met the sand, surveying the inside of the cabana.

Two inert forms lay sprawled across two of the chaise longues, and Josh released a slow breath.

He shimmied beneath the edge of the tent and army-crawled to the corner near the opening of it. Then he pulled the gun from his waistband and crouched…and waited.

This, he knew.

When rescuing damsels in distress and drugging spies, he was winging it. Lying in wait with a weapon in hand was second nature.

He'd let it slip tonight in that couple's hotel room that he was a sniper. He could tell by the look on her face Gina hadn't known that or thought about it before, but he could see the wheels start turning. Had he distracted her enough to stop the path of her thoughts?

He could probably tell Gina, without ramifications, that he'd been the one who had taken out Ricky. The way she'd felt about her husband had put him in the clear. She might even thank him, but how did you tell someone you'd killed her spouse? Taken away her child's father?

Josh tensed his muscles at the sound of scuffling sand. His hand tightened on the gun, as a shadow passed by the outside of the cabana.

The intruder led with his weapon, using it to push aside the flap of canvas covering the entrance.

Josh acted on instinct and training. He grabbed the barrel of the gun close to the handle and yanked down. The man grunted. His own instinct to hang on to his weapon caused his wrist to twist and his finger to lose its place on the trigger.

Josh brought home his advantage of surprise by driving his shoulder against the man's kneecap.

The intruder's legs buckled and as he dropped to the ground, Josh brought it home with a jab to the man's windpipe with his elbow. The guy released his gun.

Sputtering and groaning, the man only managed to suck dry sand into his mouth. He gagged and coughed.

Finally, Josh brought his own gun level with the man's forehead. "Now, you're going to tell me everything you know about who's on this island, what you want with Gina De Santos and what you think Hector De Santos hid."

The man's lips curled into a snarl. "Go to hell."

"Let's start with you." Josh kicked the man in the thigh. "Sit up."

He struggled to a seated position, and Josh patted him down, withdrawing a knife from a holster strapped to the man's leg.

"Who are you working for?"

"Not some low-life, cheating drug dealer." The man spit into the sand.

"Yeah, because a terrorist organization that targets innocent civilians is so above all that."

"There are no innocent civilians." The man's teeth gleamed in the darkness. "You should know that better than anyone. You're a sniper for one of the most lethal SEAL teams in the navy."

Josh's blood ran like ice water in his veins, and he narrowed his eyes. "Who are you? Are you working with Vlad?"

The man laughed so hard he choked. Raising his hand to his mouth, he met Josh's eyes. "He'll get his revenge. You'll never stop him."

Then he bit down on a heavy ring on his middle finger and collapsed in the sand.

Chapter Thirteen

The warm breeze lifted the ends of Gina's hair as she squinted at the ocean and a line of white-caps flashing across its inky blue surface. Gentle chatter from the pool bar rose through the night air against the backdrop of the rolling sea's rush.

She hadn't heard any gunshots, screams or general pandemonium so whatever Josh was doing down there, he was doing it quietly. Or he was dead.

She pressed her folded hands against her lurching stomach. Why had she allowed her mind to go there? Josh knew what he was doing. He had a weapon, and he knew how to use it.

In fact, he'd mentioned earlier when they were searching the hotel room that he was a sniper, a navy SEAL sniper. Had she heard that correctly?

Something bumped against the hotel room

door, and Gina spun around, her heart thumping, rattling her rib cage. She turned from the balcony and crept back in the room.

As she drew close to the door, someone tapped on it, making her jump. She pressed her eye against the peephole and released a noisy breath while flipping back the chain.

"Why are you banging around out here?" She gasped as Josh stumbled across the threshold, shirtless, his clothes and hair wet.

She slammed the door shut and threw the lock again. "Are you all right? What happened out there?"

Sluicing a hand across his hair, he tried to steady his breath as his chest heaved. "He's dead."

"The man you went to meet? How?" She knotted her fingers in front of her. If anyone saw Josh, he could be in big trouble. Isla Perdida didn't fool around with criminals, no matter what their nationality.

"He killed himself."

"I don't understand."

"I got the jump on him. He was never expecting me, and I got him at gunpoint. He…he knew who I was. When I started asking him questions, he downed some poison. He died immediately."

"Poison?" Gina took a turn around the room. "What? Where did he get poison?"

"He had it in a ring on his finger. He must've had orders to off himself if he ever got captured. I suppose if he hadn't, he would've been killed anyway. There is no way a terrorist organization is going to believe that a captive is not spilling his guts about everything he knows."

She doubled over, her hair creating a curtain around her face. "I can't believe this is happening."

"That ring? That's some serious stuff. They're prepared for anything, including death." He touched her back. "Are you okay?"

She straightened up. "Me? I've been cooling my heels in here all evening. What about you? How come you're soaking wet?"

"I couldn't leave his body there in the cabana. Maybe Roger and Tara would've taken care of business, but maybe they have similar orders. I didn't want to take any chances, so I dragged him down to the water. I hauled him over the reef. I'm hoping the current will take him out to sea, although he'll probably wash up somewhere."

"Just hopefully not before we leave. What happened to your—" she waved her hand over his glistening muscles "—shirt?"

"I figured this way, I'd just look like I went out for a late-night swim or a dip in the pool in case anyone noticed me."

"Do you think anyone did?" How could any woman in her right mind *not* notice him?

"I stayed away from the populated areas of the hotel. I avoided the lobby and the elevators and took the outside stairs."

She ducked into the bathroom and grabbed a towel for him. As she tossed it to him, she asked, "Did you get anything out of him before…?"

"Not much."

"But something?" She tilted her head to one side. Josh's face had gotten that tight look.

"He said something that confirmed a suspicion I had, that the CIA had."

"Which is?" She sat on the edge of the bed, pinning her nervous hands between her knees.

"The leader of this terrorist group is someone we know, someone I know."

"You *know* a leader of a terrorist group?" Her legs started bouncing.

"I guess *know* isn't the right word." He swiped the towel over his short hair and draped it around his neck, hanging on to it with both hands. "There was a guy, a sniper, for the other side. He was deadly accurate, and he seemed to be everywhere we were."

"By *we*, you mean…?"

"My sniper team."

She dropped her chin to her chest, letting his

words sink in. She'd been right about what he'd said before. He was not just a navy SEAL; he was a sniper—not that it made a difference. Did it?

"We got to know him, to recognize his style. We started calling him Vlad because he used a Russian sniper rifle, but in truth, we don't know what nationality he is or where his loyalties lie."

"You don't know his real name?"

"No. We know what he looks like, sort of. We've seen him, probably in disguise. He's been involved in the planning of attacks on US soil. So far we've thwarted him, but it's more than that."

Josh took his time pulling the gun from his pocket, wiping it with the towel and placing it on the credenza holding the TV. He unbuttoned the top button of his shorts and then seemed to remember where he was. He bunched up the towel and tossed it toward the open door of the bathroom.

"It's more than what? Finish the thought… out loud, please."

"I told you the man on the beach realized who I was, knew I was a SEAL."

"Yes."

"It all seems so…personal, not just this assignment but a couple of others."

"Personal? Like Vlad is devising these plans just to get to your team?"

"Yep."

"But if Vlad is the one who was working with my father to supply drugs for arms and passage into the US, he wasn't doing that to get at your team."

"No, I didn't say that. I think Vlad is going about his evil business but when his business clashes with ours—" Josh snapped his fingers "—he's ready to take his revenge."

"In a way, Vlad must feel as if you're dogging his every step."

"Tough luck for him—we are." He shrugged. "I'm going to get out of these wet shorts."

Her gaze trailed after him as he disappeared into the bathroom. He ran the shower for a few minutes, probably to rinse the sea salt and sand from his body, and she was sitting in exactly the same spot when he emerged with a whoosh of steam back into the room, a pair of running shorts hanging low on his hips.

She nibbled on the side of her thumb as she watched him dump some stuff in his suitcase and lock the gun back in the safe.

Straightening up to his full height, he glanced over his shoulder. "Are you okay? No disturbances while I was gone?"

"Everything was quiet." She crossed her legs beneath her body. "Are we ready for tomorrow?"

"I play the bodyguard, and you do what you have to do to access your father's safe-deposit box. Hopefully, we'll get lucky and find a clue to where he stashed the weapons, the drugs or both."

"I have a good feeling about this. I feel lucky."

He cocked an eyebrow at her. "After the day you just had? That's lucky?"

"Yeah, welcome to paradise." She kneaded the back of her neck with her fingers. "But I figure our luck has to change. I think it already has. If you hadn't caught on to the honeymoon couple, they would've drugged us or murdered us first."

"That's looking on the bright side." He flexed his fingers. "Do you want some help with that massage? I'm pretty good at working out the knots. God knows, my muscles get stiff when I'm watching a target for a long period of time. I've become a master at the quickie."

She hoped he meant quickie massage and not another kind of quickie because making love with Josh Elliott should be slow and languorous.

She swung her legs off the bed, perching on the edge. "Give it a try."

The mattress dipped as he sat next to her, and she turned away from him, offering him her back. Still shirtless, he exuded warmth from his body as he placed his hands on her shoulders.

"I'll start with your neck and work my way out and down. You tell me what works."

She bounced on the bed when he dug his thumbs into the sides of her neck. It hurt...and then it hurt so good.

Closing her eyes, she tilted her head to one side. "So you sit for long periods of time watching a target?"

The magic fingers stopped and she jerked her shoulders up and down to get him to start again, which he did.

"Yes, watching a target or watching a particular location for a target to appear."

"Snipers aren't in the midst of the battlefield?"

"Not generally, or you could say we're in the midst of the battlefield but doing a different type of job. We make sure areas are clear so that marines and other personnel can get their jobs done. We keep watch over them."

"And you take people out."

This time the magic fingers dug in deeper, and she winced.

"Of course, but the more bad people we take out, the more good people we save. I've always looked at it that way. It's what we do."

He stroked her shoulders, and she melted beneath his touch.

"That's what you were doing in Colombia?"

"What?"

"Making sure the area was clear for the CIA?"

Josh sighed and his warm breath tickled the back of her neck.

"Why would you do that? There was nobody to clear out of that area around my father's compound, except the people inside the compound." Her spine straightened and she jerked beneath Josh's touch. "In fact, why would a bunch of navy SEAL snipers be watching over CIA agents as they took out a group of men on the patio?"

"Gina…"

She jerked forward and whipped around. "What did you do at my father's compound, Josh?"

"I killed your husband."

Chapter Fourteen

Gina caught her breath as her heart fluttered in her chest. *Of course.*

The confident hands on her shoulders paused, the fingers entangled in her hair.

Her gaze met Josh's, unwavering, unapologetic. She'd known. She'd always known. Why would a bunch of navy SEAL snipers stand by and allow CIA agents to take down the prized targets?

She didn't even know if CIA agents killed people…but snipers did. Snipers had killed her father and her husband. Josh had killed her husband.

Confusion reigned in her mind. She opened her mouth but couldn't form one word. She slid from beneath Josh's touch and wandered to the window. Glancing at his reflection in the glass, she banished it by sliding open the door and stepping onto the balcony. She shut the door behind her, placing a barrier between them.

She inhaled the sweet scent on the air, hibiscus and jasmine mingling with the salt of the sea.

But another smell invaded her nostrils—the smell of blood and flesh and fear on the patio of her father's compound. The sounds of the servants' screams and terror echoed in her ears.

Gina covered her face with her hands. She didn't know what to feel. Why had this shadowy organization sent Josh out to monitor her? Did they figure he'd be the one to take her out if he discovered she'd picked up where her father had left off?

The way he'd rescued her from the man in the alley and the guy on the boat told a different story. He'd done nothing but protect her since the day they met…and even before.

She might not know how to feel now, but she remembered very clearly how she'd felt the day the leadership of Los Santos had been eliminated. *Relief.*

While everyone had been falling apart around her on that patio, a serene calm had descended on her shoulders. She'd felt free for the first time in months—and she owed it all to that man behind her in the hotel room.

The door slid open behind her.

"Gina?"

She dropped her hands and gripped the edge of the balcony.

"I'm sorry I didn't tell you sooner. I didn't think it was…appropriate, especially after I met RJ."

She cocked her head to the side and the lights at the pool below blurred as tears pooled in her eyes. She'd felt relief, but RJ had lost his father and his grandfather. Whatever else Hector De Santos was, he was a doting grandfather.

She smacked the balcony with her palms. Would a doting grandfather threaten to rip his grandson from his mother's arms? Would a doting grandfather make plans to inculcate his grandson in the ways of the cartel so he could take over for him in his dotage?

And what about Ricky? He'd never been an involved father. He'd always seen RJ as a pawn, a way to ingratiate himself into Hector's good graces and a solid position of power within the cartel.

Josh shuffled behind her but kept his distance. "That was always the worst part for me, depriving a child of his parent. I saw RJ before…before. I saw him with you on the patio. I wish I hadn't."

She cleared her throat. "Ricky wasn't much of a father."

"Sometimes that doesn't matter. My mother wasn't much of a mother, and I still wanted revenge for her death or at least answers."

She drew her brows over her nose and sniffed. "I think RJ's better off without his father, without his grandfather in his life. Do you feel that way about your mother?"

"I suppose. I don't know. Was Ricky abusive toward RJ?"

"If by *abusive* you mean did he smack him around? No. But if you mean did he threaten to take him from me, did he use him to get close to my father, did he bring him into dangerous situations with dangerous people? Then, yes. He was abusive, and so was my father...and I guess I was, too."

Josh was beside her in a minute. "That's not true. You didn't have a choice. If you had refused to bring him around your father, Hector De Santos would've made sure you never saw RJ again. You and I both know he could've made good on his promise. You did what you had to do."

Josh's hand rested next to hers on the railing of the balcony, and she shifted her little finger over so that it touched his. "And you did what you had to do."

He expelled a breath. "I'm thinking I should've told you sooner. I shouldn't have left it for you to figure out on your own. I guess I'm a coward."

"A coward?" She twisted her head to the right to take in the fearless man at her side. "That's not the first word or even the hundredth I'd use to describe you, Josh."

"There's no other word to explain why I didn't tell you from the start."

"Really? How about *sensitive*? I mean, who would walk up to someone and say, 'Nice to meet you, I'm the guy who killed your husband'?"

"That would be awkward." He hunched his shoulders. "But I'm not usually the most sensitive guy in the room."

"You do a pretty good impression of one."

"I didn't tell you because… I wanted you to like me. I thought maybe you still had feelings for your husband, and you'd hate me for being the one who ended his life. I didn't want you to hate me."

"Hate you?" She covered his strong hand with her own. "You saved my life. You saved RJ's life. My father planned to initiate RJ into the cartel as soon as he was old enough."

Josh cursed. "What kind of grandfather would do that? What kind of man? Your husband was on board with this?"

"Of course. Ricky figured RJ would cement

his own unbreakable bond with Los Santos. That's why Ricky wanted to have a baby with me so quickly." She snorted. "I thought it was true and undying love and the desire to create a family."

"Some people should never have children."

Josh's voice sounded hollow and she wanted nothing more than to ask him more about the mother he'd lost, but she squeezed his hand instead.

"I can't regret having RJ. He's the light of my life."

"I'm glad my role in the assassinations is out in the open." He slipped his hand from beneath hers and hunched over the balcony, folding his arms. "I'm glad you didn't love Ricky anymore."

"I stopped loving him the day he informed me that we were taking RJ to Colombia to visit my father—and RJ hadn't even been born yet. He told me then that my father had reached out to him and they'd been meeting in secret, all while I was pregnant."

"I'm sorry he betrayed you."

"You see now why I believe you saved me?" She stroked his bare back. Although Josh's role in the assassinations had come as a shock, she didn't ever want him to think she blamed him or had any regrets about Ricky's death.

His spine had stiffened beneath her touch, and her fingers played along his smooth flesh. She knew what she *would* regret at the end of this adventure with Josh. It had been a long time since she'd felt safe with any man. She needed that now.

Scraping her nails lightly along his side, she whispered, "You saved me, Josh Elliott, and you saved my son."

He turned to her and cupped her face with one hand. "Then I did my job."

She twisted her head to the side and kissed his rough palm. Then she stood on her tiptoes and kissed the base of his neck where his pulse throbbed against her lips.

His hand slipped to the back of her head, his fingers gathering her loose hair. He tugged her head back and slanted his mouth over hers.

His kiss was just a taste. It felt comforting. She didn't want comfort. She wanted the passion they'd ignited in the water this afternoon. She needed to obliterate the memory of her dead, deceitful husband. And what better way to do that than to make love with the man who'd killed him?

She hooked her arms around Josh's waist, pulling herself closer to him, her hips meeting his. She pressed against him, wanting to feel the proof of his desire for her…and he didn't disappoint.

At least below the waist, he didn't disappoint. His kiss had waned, his touch had slackened.

She sucked in his bottom lip and nibbled on it, hoping to show him she meant business… or pleasure. She slipped her hands beneath the waistband of his shorts, digging her fingers into the muscle of his buttocks.

He groaned in her ear and then growled, "Do you know what you're doing here?"

"Here in Isla Perdida or here on this balcony with a hot SEAL in my hands?"

"Either, both…ah."

His words and hopefully his reasoning trailed off as she cupped his backside with both hands and undulated against his erection.

"I know what I'm doing, and I know what I want."

He hooked his hands beneath her thighs and hoisted her up. Hiking up her dress, she wrapped her legs around his waist as he took possession of her mouth again—this time like he meant it.

With one arm braced against the balcony railing and one supporting her derriere, Josh invaded her mouth with his tongue.

She welcomed it, demanded more. She sucked

on his tongue with the same rhythm that drove her hips against his, over and over.

Her thin panties, damp with sweat and desire, chafed against her skin.

Josh reached between them and ripped them free from her body, as if sensing her discomfort...or his own.

The soft cotton of Josh's shorts stroked and tickled her bare flesh. She broke away from their kiss to gasp for breath as her blood heated up.

He rolled to his back so that the balcony railing supported him, then he gripped her thighs with both hands, his fingers sinking into her soft flesh, centimeters away from her pulsing pleasure zone.

He ran his tongue up one side of her neck and nibbled on her earlobe. His voice, harsh with pent-up desire, exploded in her ear. "You're not doing this out of gratitude, are you?"

"I can bake cookies to thank you, SEAL." She loosened her legs and yanked down his shorts, gasping at the feel of warm skin against warm skin.

During her repositioning, Josh's fingers had resettled closer to her core. Taking advantage of his new outlook, Josh plunged one finger inside her.

She threw her head back with a whimper. A

burst of laughter erupted from a gaggle of late-nighters at the pool bar below and excitement flooded every cell of her body.

She'd been weighing the best time to move this party to the bed, but now her passion flamed with the thought of making love with Josh on the balcony. Nobody could see them, but just the thought of being claimed by Josh in a semipublic place had her senses on fire.

He pulled his finger out and strategically stroked her, stoking her onto heights of passion. Her belly fluttered and her toes curled. As every muscle in her body tightened in anticipation of her release, she dug her fingernails into Josh's shoulders.

Her orgasm hit her like a wave and she trembled beneath its awesome power. As it receded, she shivered with pleasure and her limbs grew heavy and boneless until her legs slipped from Josh's body.

She had to lean against him to keep from sliding to his feet, and he caressed her backside to ease her transition from heaven to earth.

He dipped his head and kissed her jaw. "Are you ready to try out that bed?"

"I want you to take me right here." She stroked his erection, cupping him below with her other hand.

"When you touch me like that, I'll give you

anything you want. But I can't do this with you all wrapped around my body—as amazing as that feels."

He encircled her waist with both hands and did a little dance so that she was the one against the balcony, facing outward to the pool and the sea beyond.

He pulled her dress over her head and dropped it on one of the chairs. "I don't think anyone can see us up here."

He cupped her breasts with his hands, pinching her nipples, and she wriggled her bottom against him, feeling the hard tip of his erection brushing against her.

His hands played across her body, smoothing, caressing, tweaking, until her knees were trembling and she had to hold on to the railing with both hands.

He placed a hand flat on her back. "Bend forward."

She folded her arms on top of the wooden railing and gazed out at the deep blue of the water, the whitecaps drawing lines across the surface.

Josh parted her thighs and poked at her from behind, easing her open, filling her up, inch by inch. When he reached his hilt, his thighs pressing against the bare skin of her bottom, he pulled out almost all the way.

Just when she was missing him, he plunged into her again. Slow and fast he went, following some rhythm in his head, but it must've been her rhythm, too, because her passion grew with every thrust.

He slipped a hand in front of her, between her legs, and teased her again. It didn't take more than a few flicks from his fingertips before she reached her peak. This time, Josh extended her ride at the top as he plowed into her.

Her moans soon turned to cries of release and unabashed euphoria. Could they hear her down there? She didn't care. She felt alive and free for the first time in forever.

As she clenched around Josh, his thrusts grew more frenzied until he stopped and shuddered. When he was done, he wrapped his arms around her, pulling her against his chest, still inside her.

He kissed the back of her head. "Was that uncomfortable for you? I gave you what you wanted."

She pulled away from him and then turned in his arms. "You gave me more than I wanted. Was I...? Did you...?"

He put his finger to her lips. "You were everything I wanted."

He traced the pad of his finger along the red line across her belly. "It's a good thing I didn't flip you over the balcony."

"It would've been a heckuva way to go." She smoothed her hands across his chest. "I'm ready to try that bed now."

Josh wedged a finger beneath her chin and kissed her bruised lips. "After you."

When he stepped aside, Gina pushed off the balcony. A commotion from the pool deck halted her next step and she tripped into Josh.

He took her hand and they peered over the balcony, side by side. A crowd of people had formed a semicircle around a man, wet from the sea, waving his arms and pointing back toward the water.

Josh whispered, "Looks like that dead body washed up after all."

SHOWERED AND FULLY CLOTHED, Josh sat on the edge of the bed and gently prodded Gina. "Gina, it's time to get up."

It was past time, but he hadn't the heart to wake her earlier. She'd had a restless night beside him, tossing and turning and twitching in her sleep.

They hadn't made love again, although before some nighttime swimmer had discovered a dead body in the water, he'd had every intention of doing so. The reminder of what they were doing here and the high stakes involved had put a damper on their libidos.

And then the reality of what he'd succumbed to hit him full force. He was pretty sure his assignment didn't include sleeping with the widow of the man he'd killed over a year ago.

He'd been saved from making this very mistake yesterday by the man in the boat. Looked like that same man in death hadn't come along soon enough last night to prevent the same mistake.

He brushed his hand along the length of her smooth arm. How could he call what had happened between them a mistake? It had felt so natural, so right.

He'd been concerned once Gina found out he'd pulled the trigger on her husband, she'd reject him, push him away. Instead she'd turned to him in gratitude.

As much as she'd denied her motivation, he could sense it in the urgency of her touch. It made sense—for her. He didn't have to go along for the ride. He traced the curve of her ear with his fingertip. But what a ride it had been.

No red-blooded American male would've been able to resist a hot-blooded Gina De Santos. He didn't claim to have any willpower in that area.

Maybe Ariel and the folks pulling the strings already knew that and were counting on it. How much easier would it be to manipulate a woman once you'd gotten her into your bed?

Somehow *he* felt like the manipulated one. He'd been dreading tears and anger when he'd broken the news about his role in Ricky's demise. When she'd responded with relief and understanding, he still felt he owed her something. If she preferred her payment in the currency of his kisses, who was he to deny her?

But it was back to business today.

"Gina?" He brushed the hair from her face and kissed her sweet mouth.

Like Sleeping Beauty, she roused, blinking her eyes and rubbing a hand across her mouth. "It's morning?"

"The bank opens in thirty minutes."

She bolted upright, the covers falling from her naked shoulders. "Thirty minutes? Why didn't you get me up sooner?"

"The bank's open for four hours. We have plenty of time." His gaze lingered on her perfect breasts, so soft and full they made his mouth water all over again.

She yanked the sheet up to her chin. "I have to get ready."

"The bathroom is all yours." He flicked the collar of his white button-down shirt. "As you can see, I'm ready to roll."

"We won't have time for breakfast."

"We'll get some later. Our flight isn't until late afternoon."

She rolled from the bed, dragging the covers with her in a sudden attack of modesty.

He'd seen—and touched—it all last night. She wasn't hiding anything from him now. Did she have regrets, too? Maybe she'd paid her debt and wanted to move on.

She rummaged in her suitcase, grabbed a few items and headed for the bathroom, calling over her shoulder, "I won't be long."

Josh shook out his jacket and draped it over the back of the chair. Isla Perdida might have its tourist and resort areas, but the island took its business very seriously.

He cranked on the air-conditioning and closed the door to the balcony, throwing a cursory glance at the pool. He'd meandered downstairs for coffee this morning and had picked up a few bits of info. A guest at the hotel had found a man floating in the sea, several yards from the beach. No immediate evidence of foul play had led to initial reports of a drowning.

Josh could live with that story for the rest of their stay on the island. The toxicology report would soon refute a simple drowning, but the authorities just might rule suicide—and they'd be correct.

If his followers preferred suicide to capture

and questioning, Vlad must have some devoted minions—devoted or terrified.

The bathroom door banged open behind him and Gina squealed, "It's freezing in here."

"Wait until you put on your bank duds. I don't want to melt out of the suit before I even leave the room."

"You have a point." She eyed the white dress hanging in the closet with something like trepidation in every muscle.

She dropped the towel she'd been hugging to her chest to reveal a snow-white set of bra and panties. She yanked the dress from the hanger and stepped into it, reaching around to her back to pull up the zipper.

"Let me." He crossed the room and slid the dress closed over her smooth mocha skin.

Gina had needed just one day in the blistering, relentless sun to sport an even tan across her body. He'd enjoyed tracing her tan lines last night, and had enjoyed exploring beyond the tan lines even more.

"Thanks." She stepped away from him and into a pair of beige high-heeled sandals. "At least *I'm* not expected to wear a suit."

"Lucky." He planted himself in front of the mirror and buttoned his top button. Then he reached for the tie hanging over the lid of his open suitcase.

"Do you need help with that?" She pointed at the blue tie hanging from his fingertips.

He raised his brows at the image he presented in the mirror, noticing the way his white shirt bunched around his shoulders and arms. Last time he wore this getup was for a buddy's funeral. Thank God, he hadn't needed it since, but he'd pumped up a bit more since then.

"Don't I look like the suit-and-tie type?"

"You look…just fine."

He held it out to her. "I could use some help."

She looped the tie over his head and tucked it beneath the collar of his shirt. "I know just one knot, so I hope you like it."

He dropped his gaze to hers. "I like everything you do."

She pressed her lips together but they twitched at the corner. Then she lodged the tip of her tongue in that same corner as she fed one end of the tie through an opening and flipped it over the other end.

"I think I got this." She turned him toward the mirror. "What do you think? Straighten it out a bit from your angle."

"Looks great." He tightened the knot. "Are you ready?"

"I need some makeup and I'm going to do my hair, so cool your heels for another fifteen minutes."

"I can't imagine how your face could look any more beautiful with fifteen minutes of makeup application."

This time her lips turned down in a frown. "You're very free and easy with the compliments this morning."

He sucked in his bottom lip. He'd never been accused of that before. The flattery just seemed to spring to mind, but whatever was prompting him to sing her praises, Gina didn't seem to like it.

Had Ricky Rojas laid it on thick? He'd probably wooed and schmoozed her as if his life depended on it. He'd seemed like a smooth SOB, just the kind of guy women would fall for—especially young and inexperienced ones like Gina had been.

"I'll zip it if it makes you uncomfortable." He held up his hands. "Wait. That didn't come out right."

She gave him a nervous giggle. "That's okay. Who doesn't like compliments?"

"Nobody likes them if they're not sincere." He drew a cross over his heart. "I swear, mine are completely spontaneous and sincere. Can't you tell by how clunky they are?"

"They're not." She nudged him away from the mirror and pulled her hair back.

He retreated to a chair and sat on the edge,

watching Gina as she wound her luxuriant dark hair into a severe bun at the back of her head. "Are you nervous?"

"A little, but I have all the valid qualifications to get into my father's safe-deposit box." She stuck a pin in her hair and smoothed her hands over the skirt of her dress. "We should be fine."

She held up a small leopard-print bag. "Just some makeup and I'll be ready to go."

For this particular operation Gina went into the bathroom, and he stood up and lifted his jacket from the chair. They'd take a taxi for the ten-minute ride into town.

When Gina emerged from the bathroom with her war paint on, she did look ready to do battle—beautiful, sophisticated, just a little brittle.

"You look…ready."

"Let's do this."

"If it all comes to nothing…"

"It won't." She sliced a hand in the air right in front of his nose. "I got to know my father pretty well in those last months of his life. I had to study him to figure out a way to escape my predicament. This is what he'd do. This is where he'd keep his secrets."

"We'll soon find out, one way or the other." He draped his jacket over his arm, feeling for the gun in the pocket.

They made their way down to the lobby and

as they traversed the gold-threaded marble, Josh made a detour to the front desk.

He ducked his head and asked the hotel clerk, "Is it true there was a dead body on the beach last night?"

Gina tensed beside him.

"Yes, sir, but no violence. No violence on the island. It looks to be a drowning." He shrugged. "Some shouldn't go out swimming at night in the dark."

"I'll keep that in mind." He rapped on the counter. "Thank you."

Gina let out a breath. "That's the word, huh? A drowning?"

"It is until the coroner runs a toxicology report, but we'll be long gone before those results come in."

"They're going to have a hard time finding his next of kin since he probably was using a fake name, unless the newlywed couple wants to claim him."

"Not likely."

The front doors of the hotel whisked open at their approach, and a bellhop jumped to attention. "Taxi, sir?"

"Yes, please."

The bellhop whistled and waved, and a hybrid car rolled up to the curb.

Josh gave the bank name to the driver. No address was necessary.

The taxi silently sped along the main road that wended its way around the island. Unlike Robbie from the day before, this driver made no small talk. In a place like Isla Perdida, small talk with people heading to the Banco de Perdida could get you in trouble.

At the end of the short drive, the cabbie hopped out of his car and opened the back door. Josh paid him and added a generous tip—in case anyone came around later asking about their destination and conversation. It was standard practice on the island.

Josh kept his hands to himself as he followed Gina into the bank, just like any good bodyguard would do. Any good bodyguard would decline to sleep with his charge, too.

Guess he was a failure as a bodyguard.

Josh opened the door of the bank and the cold air blasted his face. Were they afraid all their money might melt in the island heat?

An armed security guard stepped forward. "Your business, please?"

Gina flashed the passbook, green leather embossed with gold, from her father. "I'm here to visit my safe-deposit box. This is my bodyguard."

Josh placed his hand inside the pocket of his

jacket just so there were no misunderstandings later.

The security guard nodded and gestured toward one of the small teller windows at the end of the row.

Gina's heels clicked on the marble floor and echoed among the hush of soft whispers emanating from the edges of the room.

Josh inhaled the scent of what had to be pure money...or maybe it was the smell of gold bullion.

Gina parked herself in front of the window and he hovered to her right as she whipped out various forms of ID, including pressing her thumb to an electronic pad.

She must've had everything in order because the teller at the window told her to proceed to the gated entrance to the left of the windows.

Josh followed Gina to the locked doors and they both waited while someone on the other side released a series of locks and opened the door.

Gina jerked her thumb over her shoulder. "He's my bodyguard."

The bank official nodded and stepped aside. It was even more hushed on this side of the windows and more discreet. The black-suited official led them to the safe-deposit area and entered a code on the door. Gina then entered her code, which she'd memorized from a card in the taxi, and the door clicked open.

"Take your time, Ms. De Santos." The clerk melted away instead of sticking around like most bankers did for safe-deposit boxes in the United States.

When the door swung shut behind them in the dimly lit room lined with boxes of various sizes, Josh said, "I suppose it's better for the people who work here to be kept in the dark as to the contents of these boxes."

Gina released a breath as if she'd been holding it since they walked into the bank. "That's why the rich and crooked bank here—total privacy."

"I suppose your father didn't have a box big enough to hold drugs and weapons."

"I don't think so." She floated past the wall of boxes, trailing her fingers along their gleaming brass fronts. "I remember being in here with my father like it was yesterday. I was terrified then by the implications, but now I'm glad he entrusted all this to me."

"You're going to have to entrust this to the DEA when this is all over."

She shrugged. "I'll have to tell my mom first. She may lose everything."

"It was never hers to lose, Gina. Does she want blood on her hands?"

"My mother wants cash in her hands, whether it has blood on it or not. Do you really think she didn't know my father's profession when she married him? She did." She stopped about two-thirds of the way down the row. "Here it is."

She wiped her palms against the skirt of her dress, and then punched in a code. The lock on the box clicked, and Gina pulled the box from its cavity.

She placed it on the table in the middle of the room and flipped up the felt lid.

Josh leaned over her shoulder as she picked up a folded batch of papers and dropped them on the table.

Whistling, he hooked his finger around a diamond necklace and two matching bracelets. "I'm no expert, but these look like they could fund a few small wars."

"I have no idea why these are in here." She picked up a stack of American bills. "Or these."

"No secret tapes, computer disks, DVDs?" He dropped the necklace and bracelets on top of the papers and stirred his finger among a few other pieces of jewelry in the felt-lined box.

"Doesn't look like it."

"What about these?" Josh tapped the papers that had been on top.

Gina picked up the batch of papers, tipping them to the side, letting the diamonds slide to the table in a glittering pool. She unfolded them and flattened them on the table with her palms.

"I don't know what this is supposed to be." She leaned over the eleven-by-fifteen sheets of paper and ran her fingertip along the lines on the page.

Josh bumped the side of her hip with his own to get a closer look. "These are plans, some kind of building plans with measurements and calculations."

"My father was never into real estate or buildings as far as I know. Why would he even be interested in building plans? It's not his compound in Colombia, is it?"

Josh squinted at the numbers, and then dug in his pocket for his phone. He entered some of the figures on his phone's calculator, and drew his brows over his nose. "This can't be a building. Those numbers are too small. The ceiling's barely six feet tall."

"My father was not a tall man, but the ceilings in his place were super high—cathedral."

"Are these more plans?" Josh shoved aside the top page only to find another odd set of figures. "We're going to need an architect to look at these, or at least someone with more building experience than I have."

He thumbed through the next few pages.

When he came to the last one, his heart flip-flopped. "Gina, it's a map."

"Like a buried treasure map?" Bending forward, she dug her elbows into the table and peered at the squiggly lines on the page.

"It's Mexico." Josh's adrenaline started pumping, and a bead of sweat ran down his face despite the arctic temperatures in the room.

Gina wrinkled her nose. "Why Mexico?"

"Think about it." Josh jabbed the map with his finger. "This is the border with the US."

Gina's mouth dropped open, her eyes alight with understanding. "The crossing."

"Right." Josh scrabbled back through the other pages and grabbed the edges of the first set of plans. His gaze darted from one side of the page to the other, as calculations whirred through his brain.

Then he dropped the plans on the table with a pump of his fist. "This is it. You were right, Gina."

"I was? What do you think you figured out?"

"I don't *think* I figured it out. I *know* I did. Your father commissioned the construction of a tunnel between Mexico and the US and that's where he hid the drugs and the weapons. And they must still be there."

Chapter Fifteen

Josh's words acted like a switch to a light bulb over her head. How else would her father be able to secure passage for the terrorists and their weapons in exchange for drugs?

"You're right. It's all here in front of us." She picked up the edges of the map and read off some of the names. "It's at the border with Arizona. Can you figure out the exact location?"

"I'm sure we can once we compare this map to another. When I turn this over to the team, to Ariel, the CIA and the DEA can move in and confiscate the drugs and the weapons and destroy the tunnel. I wonder if it's been used yet. There are dozens of these tunnels on the border. I wonder what makes this one so special. I'm sure Los Santos has used tunnels before to ship their drugs to the States."

"I'm not sure. I wasn't aware of any tunnels before." Gina chewed on her bottom lip as Josh laid out each of the pages on the table. "Once this tunnel is located and if the drugs and weapons are there, do you think these people—Los Santos and this Vlad guy—will leave me alone?"

Josh looked up from taking his first picture of the plans with his phone. "They should. They tried to abduct you to get information from you and get you to turn it over to them. They failed."

"Thanks to you."

"Don't get too warm and fuzzy. I was sent to Miami, to you, to get the exact same information."

"Yeah, but you're the good guys." She wedged a hip against the table, watching Josh as he finished taking his pictures. "If I hadn't had the info or wouldn't turn it over to you, I don't think the US government's response would've been the same as Los Santos's or Vlad's."

"You sure about that?" He shifted his gaze from his phone to her face. "If we knew you had information that you weren't coughing up? It could've gotten ugly."

Gina narrowed her eyes as Josh collected the papers and folded them along their original seams. Could've gotten ugly or very, very friendly? Had Ariel and the powers that be told him to get to her using any means possible?

Her lips twitched at the idea of Josh as some

kind of Mata Hari using his masculine wiles to woo information from her. She'd been the one who'd been all over him last night anyway. She doubted he would've made a move if she hadn't come on to him.

Of course, he could've just made it seem that way.

It didn't matter. She always planned to give him any information she had about her father and she'd wanted his body anyway. It was a win-win-win for everyone.

If she could only shake this feeling that finding this tunnel wouldn't be the end of the threat against her. She'd been living under a noxious miasma of evil for so long, she didn't feel as if she'd ever be free of it.

Josh pocketed his phone and handed her the plans. "Stick these in your bag. We'll get them to the right people when we hit stateside."

She shoved the papers in her bag and picked up the diamond necklace, dangling it from her fingertips. It threw rainbow sparks around the room. "Should we leave this here for the DEA, or do you have some woman in your life who needs a fabulous gift?"

He raised his eyebrows at her. "I have no woman in my life. Didn't I make that clear last night?"

Two spots of heat lit up her cheeks. "I didn't mean… I meant like a mother or… I'm sorry."

"Like an aunt or sister or grandmother? I have no one…like that."

She dropped the jewels in the safe-deposit box. "Then the DEA gets them."

Josh scooped them back up and dropped them in his pocket. "Maybe your mother wants them. Maybe they belong to her."

"You just said none of my father's money belonged to her."

"Forget what I said. Put the box away and let's get out of here. We have a flight to catch at four o'clock and I'm never gonna feel so happy to leave paradise as when that plane lifts off."

Fifteen minutes later, after going through the steps of securing the safe-deposit box and exiting the bank, they emerged onto the sidewalk.

Blinking in the harsh sunlight, Gina shook out her sunglasses and put them on. She surveyed the empty street. "Maybe we should've called for a taxi inside the bank."

As if by magic, a yellow cab glided up to the curb. The driver wasn't as attentive as the one who'd dropped them off, staying securely behind the wheel as Josh opened the car door for her.

Josh leaned forward slightly. "La Perdida Resort and Spa, *por favor*."

As the taxi rolled into the street, another taxi pulled up behind them, horn honking.

Their driver cursed and made a rude gesture out the window.

"What is that guy's problem? We didn't cut him off." Gina twisted her head around to glare at the other driver, who was still gesticulating and honking.

Josh had turned around, too, and his body stiffened, the muscles in the thigh beneath her hand coiling.

She jerked her head toward him, and he leaned in to kiss her cheek. Before he drew away, he whispered in her ear. "We need to get out of this taxi the next time he stops or slows down."

She blinked. Slows down? Josh expected her to jump out of a moving car in a white linen dress and high-heeled sandals?

He did. His right hand rested on the door handle of the car, his left gripped her wrist. He'd drag her out if he had to.

What had he seen in the other taxi that had led him to that conclusion? The car was still behind them, the driver tailgating them.

She scooted closer to Josh, her thigh pressing against his. Reaching down, she flicked off the ankle straps of her sandals and tucked them into the big bag at her feet—right next to the map of the tunnel. She pulled the bag into her lap, and hooked the strap over her shoulder.

Josh nodded.

Their taxi slowed to take a curve to the right, and Josh pinched her wrist. As soon as he opened that door, it was go time.

Go time arrived within a nanosecond as Josh pushed open the door, yanking on her wrist. She didn't need any more prompting than that.

Josh jumped out of the taxi while the driver yelled. With Josh still holding on to her wrist, Gina hoisted herself into the space right behind him, squashing her bag against her chest.

Josh had timed their exit well. They both tumbled into a patch of crawling vines on a soft shoulder, rolling just a few feet.

Their taxi screamed to a stop several yards ahead of them. The driver bolted from the car, a gun clutched in his hand.

Gina didn't know whether to make a run for it or stay down.

Josh shoved her behind his body as he reached for his own weapon and made the decision for her. "Stay down. Burrow beneath these vines if you can."

As Josh raised his gun, the taxi that had been dogging them screeched to a halt, cutting off their view of the driver with the gun.

Before she had time to think, Josh grabbed

her upper arm and practically dragged her to the waiting taxi. A sharp report and the sound of cracking glass accompanied her into the back seat of the other taxi.

With the back door still gaping open, their new ride swung around in a wild U-turn and lurched into high speed, the sound of another gunshot behind them.

Once the taxi had gained traction and Gina had shoved the hair from her face, the driver turned around with a gold tooth gleaming in his big smile.

"*Dios mío*. Some crazy business you two are involved in."

Gina fell back against the seat. "Robbie? What are you doing here? How did you know that driver had a gun?"

Robbie looked in his rearview mirror and made a quick right turn. "I remembered Josh telling me about your appointment today at the bank. I was in the area and thought I'd roll by to give you a lift. When I saw you get into that rogue taxi, I knew you'd be in some kind of trouble."

"You have no idea." Josh clapped Robbie on the shoulder.

Gina asked, "Rogue taxi?"

"Like any place, Isla Perdida has unlicensed taxi drivers. They're especially common around the banks. They do a pickup—" Robbie made his fingers into a gun "—and then they rob you of the valuables you just collected at the bank."

Gina hugged her bag to her chest and slid a glance at Josh. "You mean that driver was just trying to rob us?"

"Just?" He shook his head. "He had a gun, senorita. He was serious, but this problem isn't something you're going to read in the guide-books or in your business plans. The island keeps such things quiet."

"Thanks for the rescue, Robbie." Josh entwined his fingers with Gina's on the seat between them.

Robbie laughed. "I think you could've handled things, Josh, especially with the little beauty *mi primo* sold to you last night, but tourists don't want to be involved in any shootings in Isla Perdida."

"We appreciate everything you've done for us, Robbie."

"It was nothing." Robbie waved his hand at the mirror. "Now, I take you to my home so my wife can look after your injuries."

"Injuries?" Gina looked Josh up and down and except for a missing button on his jacket and a few leaves stuck to his hair, he looked just fine.

"You, not me." Josh touched a finger to her cheek and showed her the blood on the end of it.

She gasped. "Is it bad?"

"No worse than your hand and arm."

As soon as the words left his mouth, she felt stinging prickles on the palm of her left hand and noticed the red abrasions for the first time. "I honestly didn't even feel those. I'm sure I'll be okay."

"Perhaps, senorita, but it's better not to return to your hotel looking like you jumped from a moving car."

"You're probably right." She tilted her head back against the seat and rolled it to the left where she saw a different type of scenery flashing by.

Tangled roadside bushes had replaced the manicured landscaping. Old clunkers were rattling down the road instead of the gleaming taxis and high-end rentals of the city streets. People were lined up at shacks with thatched roofs and smoke rising from the back instead of four-star eateries.

She hadn't seen this side of Isla Perdida on her previous visit.

"If you're hungry, I'm sure my wife has some lunch prepared for my break."

Josh said, "We don't want to put her out."

"No trouble, senor. Since our three oldest left

the island for Miami, she's been complaining she has nobody to cook for."

"Well, I'm starving." Gina brushed some dirt from her dress and then clutched the wrinkled material in her fists. "That other driver is not going to retaliate against you, is he?"

"I'd like to see him try. The *policía* don't look kindly upon the rogue drivers. Gives the island a black eye." He swung down an unpaved road with palm trees and lush vegetation on either side.

He parked the taxi in front of a tidy clapboard house with abundant fruit trees on one side and neat rows of vegetables and herbs on the other.

When Gina stepped out of the car, the moist earth squished between her toes as she inhaled the sweet scent of the blossoming fruit trees. "Now, *this* is paradise."

A petite, dark woman opened the door with a smile as big as her husband's. "*Hola, hola.* Robbie, you brought guests for lunch?"

Robbie introduced them to his wife, Fernanda, and then spoke in rapid Spanish to her, explaining about the rogue taxi driver.

She clicked her tongue. "Thieves. Come in, come in. Look at your pretty dress."

"I'm afraid it's a mess."

Fernanda tended to Gina's cuts and scrapes and then fed them a hearty meal of arroz con pollo.

An hour later, Josh tapped Gina on the shoulder, just as she'd launched probably the fiftieth picture of RJ on her phone to show Fernanda. "We should be getting back. We have a flight to catch."

Robbie stood up and stretched. "I'll take you back to the hotel and wait for you, Josh. Then I'll drive you to the airport. We need to get you out of Isla Perdida alive."

His light tone and chuckle at the end of his sentence didn't match his somber expression and tight mouth. Had Josh told him more, or had he figured it out on his own?

They said their goodbyes to Fernanda, promising to return for a visit.

Robbie got them back to the hotel without incident, and they hurriedly packed and changed clothes.

Gina turned to Josh. "You don't believe that rogue taxi driver was working for his own interests, do you?"

"Not a chance. They know we got something out of that bank, and they want their hands on it."

She snapped her suitcase shut and placed a hand over the knot in her belly. "All we need to do is get on that plane and get back to Miami."

"That's all. Easy."

Robbie made good time to the airport and

also took precautions that they weren't followed. Even if Josh hadn't given him any more details about the purpose of their visit, Robbie knew there was more to their troubles than an island thief.

He stopped his taxi in front of their terminal and hauled their bags from the trunk.

Gina gave Robbie a hug and Josh slipped him some cash with a handshake.

As Robbie started to get into his car, Josh jogged around to the driver's side. "Forgot your tip."

He plunged his hand into the pocket of his cargo shorts and pulled out his fist. Then he poured the diamonds into Robbie's hand.

Robbie's eyes bulged out of their sockets. "Josh, Josh."

"Keep them." Josh hustled back to the curb and took Gina's arm. "Let's get out of here."

As they waited in the boarding area, Gina glanced around but didn't see anyone suspicious. The honeymooners hadn't looked suspicious either.

She and Josh passed the uneventful flight back to Miami reading and studying the various passengers. The calm put her nerves on edge.

Resting her chin against Josh's arm, Gina asked, "Why aren't they coming at us now?"

"We don't know that they aren't. Stay alert.

Roger and Tara didn't look like much of a threat, did they?"

She snorted. "They didn't end up being much of a threat. *They* should've stayed alert. Amateurs."

He pinched her chin. "Let's hope you don't become a pro at this."

"It's too late." She rubbed her eyes. "I thought my life of looking over my shoulder and walking on eggshells was over when my father and Ricky died."

"Your father left you some legacy by taking you into his confidence. Others must've known or Ricky blabbed. Otherwise, you wouldn't be in this predicament. These two groups who are trying to get to the drugs and weapons would've looked elsewhere for their answers."

"Hector De Santos—the father who keeps on giving." She tugged on the sleeve of his T-shirt. "Do I have to tell the DEA about my mother's account in that same bank on Isla Perdida?"

"I'm not here to do the DEA's job. You do what you think is best."

She covered her face with her hands. "There's what's best for my mother and what's right."

The plane touched down in Miami just thirty minutes late, and they moved through Customs with their fake IDs without incident. As the escalator brought them down to the baggage claim, Gina jerked her head in the direction of a brightly colored commotion to her right.

"What the heck is my mom doing here?"

"Where?"

Gina pointed to her mother, swathed in a hot-pink ensemble, her red hair permed and coiffed, and waved. "God, she probably wants all the details of our trip."

"Maybe she just wanted to bring RJ to meet you."

Gina scanned the area around her mother and her chest tightened. "Except RJ's not with her."

"Playdate?"

"You're right." Gina huffed out a breath. "I think that was scheduled for today, even though it's a little late for that now."

The escalator deposited them onto the linoleum floor, and Gina's mom rushed toward her, hands outstretched. "Gina, Gina."

Gina's heart dropped, and the blood rushed to her head. "What's wrong, Mom?"

Her mother looked over her shoulder. "Not here."

"Where's RJ?"

Mom practically dragged her toward some plastic chairs lined up against the wall across from the baggage service windows.

"Mom, you're scaring me. Just tell me RJ's okay and we can get to the rest."

"That's just it, Gina. RJ's not okay."

Gina sank to a chair and would've missed it if Josh hadn't guided her into it.

"I-is he hurt? Mom?" She felt like screaming as a cold dread crept through her body.

"No, or at least I don't think so."

"Just tell me what happened."

"Oh, Gina, they took him. He's gone."

Chapter Sixteen

Gina doubled over and the beige floor rushed toward her face. Once again, Josh caught her by wrapping his arm around her and pulling her against his side.

"What happened, Joanna?" He reached out and pulled her mom into the chair next to him. "Start from the beginning."

"I'm so sorry, Gina. I—I don't know what I could've done differently. You said it was okay."

Gina parted her dry lips but no sound came out.

Josh's low voice sounded very faraway. "What was okay? Try to focus, Joanna, and tell us what happened."

"It was the playdate. It was just a playdate, Gina. You told me it was all right, didn't you? To arrange a playdate with that boy, Diego? He'd been to our house before."

"Is that where he is, Joanna? With Diego's parents?"

"I called the mother, Rita, very nice lady. I even dropped RJ off at their house. Diego was right there to meet him."

"Do you have the address of the house?"

"Of course, I do, but it won't do you any good. There's nobody at that house now."

Gina took a few short breaths. "Did they contact you, Mom? Or did you just go back to the house to pick him up?"

Her mother licked her frosted lips. "They contacted me before the playdate was even supposed to be over. They told me... I don't know. Craziness. They wanted me to meet you at the airport and break the news right away, but they told me not to call the police or..."

A sob bubbled up in Gina's throat. "Or they'd kill him?"

"They're not going to do that." Josh squeezed the back of Gina's neck. "If they did that, they wouldn't get what they wanted."

"Money?" Mom grabbed Josh's wrist. "I have that. I have plenty of that. They can have it all. Jewelry, too."

"They don't want money, Mom." Gina pinned Josh with her gaze. "They want something Dad left behind."

"That bastard. He just won't go away, will

he?" Mom caught a tear on the end of her manicured nail before it ran a course through her makeup. "I'm sorry, sweetie. What can I do?"

"You're going to give us all the information you can about this couple or this woman and the house." Josh pushed to his feet and offered his hands to both Gina and her mom. "You didn't call the police, did you, Joanna?"

"You think I'm stupid?" She brushed his hand aside and stood up, tottering on her five-inch heels. "Let's go get RJ back."

They piled into Mom's car, but she couldn't drive and talk at the same time because she kept getting too excited and veering into other lanes.

Josh, his skin a few shades paler than when they'd stepped off the plane, grabbed the steering wheel at one point. "Joanna, pull over. I'll drive. You talk. Gina, are you doing okay back there?"

"Just great. My son is missing and it's my fault." Her stomach lurched and she felt like she was going to be sick.

Mom pulled over, and she and Josh switched places.

At the wheel and in control, Josh started the interrogation. "What's the address of the house where you dropped off RJ? We're going there right now."

"Sh-shouldn't we take my mother home first?"

"No way. She's our guide. She can tell us everything that went down. It might lead to something."

Joanna twisted in her seat. "I want to go back, Gina, and I don't know why you're blaming yourself. How could you possibly know that woman was with Los Santos? She had such nice shoes."

Gina rocked back and forth. "You don't understand."

Josh interrupted them, "Joanna, the address."

Mom swiped a finger across her phone and read out an address.

After Josh had Gina put the address in her phone's GPS, which momentarily stopped her thoughts from sinking into the dark corners of her mind, he continued with Joanna, "What did Diego's mom look like?"

Gina nodded as her mother described the tall Latina with a short, dark chestnut bob.

"That's the same woman I met at Sunny Days."

"You tried her phone number again, Joanna?"

"Out of service."

"Was there anyone at the house besides Rita and Diego?"

"A maid." Joanna described this woman, but Gina had never seen her before at the daycare.

"Only Rita ever picked up Diego. How did Diego seem? Scared? Weird in any way?"

"How would I know? That's the first time I ever saw the kid since I wasn't home when he came over. Seemed like a normal kid to me, happy to see RJ. I wasn't there long enough to observe his interactions with the two women, but he did seem to hover around the so-called maid more, so maybe that's his real mother. That Rita didn't seem like much of a mother to me."

"You just said she was nice, Mom."

"That was before the bitch took my grandson."

"Josh, Diego started just a few days after RJ at that daycare. They must've been planning something like this as a backup."

"A backup to what?" Mom drummed her long fingernails on the dashboard. "What's going on here, and who are you, Josh?"

"I'm… Let's just say I'm working for the government. I'm trying to help Gina."

"Haven't done a very good job of that so far, have you? But then if you're with some government agency, that doesn't surprise me."

"Mom." Gina rolled her eyes at Josh in the rearview mirror. "Josh has done more than enough to help me. You have no idea. And now he's going to help us get RJ back. Isn't that right, Josh?"

"We'll find him, and whoever took him is going to pay."

Gina pressed her forehead against the window. It had remained unspoken between them, but there was no way right now that they could turn over her father's map and plans to the tunnel to Josh's superiors. How RJ's kidnappers would even know whether or not they found the information and turned it over, she wasn't sure, but she wasn't willing to take any chances with RJ's life. She hoped Josh wouldn't either.

Following the GPS directions, Josh pulled to a stop in front of a white Mediterranean with a manicured lawn and landscaped gardens.

"Looks like Rita and her pals spared no expense." Gina tapped on the window.

Josh cut the engine. "Did they come out to greet you?"

"Yes. Rita came out first, and then the maid holding the little boy's hand. He broke right away from her when he saw RJ. I said goodbye to him, and then the maid ushered them into the house." Joanna sniffed.

"Mom, what made you think this other woman was the maid? Was she wearing some kind of uniform?"

"No. I don't know why I thought that. She didn't look anything like Rita and we weren't introduced, so I didn't think she was a relative and she was too young to be Diego's grandmother."

"Let's see if we can get inside the house." Josh opened his car door.

Gina shot out of the back seat and ran to the front door. She banged on the double doors and laid on the doorbell.

Joanna put one foot on the bottom step, tapping the toe of her sandal. "Do you think I didn't try that?"

Josh cupped a hand over his eyes and tried to peer through the frosted glass next to the door. "Did you ever get inside the house, Joanna?"

"No." She twisted the rings on her fingers. "I suppose I should've. I should've demanded to see where they were going to play and who was going to be there."

"That's just hindsight, Mom." Gina sat heavily on the top step. "I don't think I would've done that at a playdate where I'd already seen the mom and some nanny or housekeeper with the kids. Don't blame yourself."

"That's the first time you've ever told me not to take the blame for everything that went wrong in your life. You even blamed me for liking Ricky Rojas. I'm not the one who married that pretty boy."

"No, you just married a drug dealer."

"So did you."

"Ladies." Josh held up his hands as if he were refereeing a prizefight. "We don't have time to open old wounds right now. I'm going around to the back of the house. You can join me or sit here and argue on the front porch."

Joanna jabbed her finger at Josh's back. "Listen to this one. He's no pretty boy."

Gina rose to her feet with a flounce, mad at herself for taking her mother's bait and appearing immature in front of Josh.

He was right. They had no time for this. RJ was gone and she knew exactly what would be asked of them to get him back. She was more than willing to hand over the plans, the map and even the diamonds if Robbie didn't have them.

But was Josh?

She knew the people pulling Josh's strings didn't give a hoot about RJ or her…but Josh did.

As she followed Josh along the side of the big house, she paused each time he checked the windows or studied the moist ground.

He opened an unlocked gate to the backyard and held it open for her and her mother, who'd slipped out of her high-heeled sandals.

Gina shivered when she caught sight of the shimmering pool, no safety gate surrounding it. Even if this playdate hadn't been totally fake, this would not have been a good environment for RJ. She'd been so vigilant about RJ ever since his birth, it had felt so normal and natural to slack off a bit and give the kid some breathing room—but she'd been too negligent.

"Here we go." Josh had crouched down in front of the sliding doors to the patio.

Gina hovered over him, his fingers tracing a neat square of cut-out glass. "They broke into this house? Isn't that taking a huge risk?"

"They probably knew it was vacant." He reached his arm inside the space and flicked the inside lock on the door. He slid it open and gestured to Gina to stay back.

He crept into the house while she and Mom waited outside.

Her mother put her hands on her hips. "Are you gonna tell me who he is now?"

"He told you."

"Is he DEA? Are you working with them now?" Her mother narrowed her eyes. "Where did the two of you go? I know it wasn't some romantic getaway in the Bahamas."

Gina's cheeks prickled with heat when she recalled making love with Josh on the balcony. It had been the most romantic and passionate thing she'd done in years… And while she'd been throwing all caution to the wind, someone was planning RJ's kidnapping.

"I can't tell you anything, Mom."

Josh poked his head outside. "It's all clear, but it doesn't look like they left anything behind."

Gina followed him inside with her mother trailing after her. Her gaze darted around the sparsely furnished room. Even if Mom had come inside, she might not have noticed anything amiss.

"It looks like show furniture. When Realtors are selling a house that's vacant, they furnish it just for show."

"I should've demanded they let me in." Joanna dropped her shoes to the tile floor and kicked one. "I would've smelled a rat."

"Maybe, maybe not." Josh stepped into the kitchen and opened the refrigerator, the empty shelves glaring back at them. "Did you notice a car out front?"

"Black Mercedes, but don't ask me the model or license number."

"Gina, did you ever see the car at daycare?"

"Never noticed."

Mom flapped her arms, looking like a giant, exotic bird. "Are you going to call...whoever?"

Gina's eyes darted toward Josh, her tongue sweeping her lower lip. Josh hadn't had a chance to tell anyone about the tunnel plans yet. If he did so now, it would be game over...for RJ and for her.

"We're going to wait." Josh leaned against the

fridge. "RJ's abductors want something from us in exchange for RJ, and we're going to give it to them—on our terms."

Gina folded her arms across her queasy stomach. She didn't like the sound of that. Terrorists had RJ in their clutches. As far as she was concerned, they could dictate any terms they wanted and she'd follow through with every one of them.

"D-do you think they'll call?"

"They have your phone number. They've made that clear already. They'll be in touch."

Joanna stamped one bare foot. "Who is *they*? Are you talking about Los Santos? Did Hector leave you something they want?"

"Something like that, Mom, but it's best you don't know anything. Can you stay with your boyfriend for a while until we get this sorted out?"

"You're kicking me out of my own home?"

"Since when did I have to twist your arm to spend time with Tom?"

As they walked back to the car, Joanna grabbed Gina's arm. "Tell me you don't blame me for this."

Gina squeezed her mom's hand. "Not at all."

She knew where the blame lay, squarely on her own shoulders.

JOSH LET OUT a breath when he loaded the last of Joanna's many suitcases into the trunk of her car, and Joanna pulled away with a wiggle of her manicured fingers.

Massaging his temples, he walked Gina back into the pastel-colored building.

"I'm sorry you had to witness all that between us." Gina stabbed the elevator call button until it arrived and they got in. "We get at each other's throats sometimes."

"It's totally understandable. You're both under a tremendous amount of stress."

"That's a nice way to put it." She rested her forehead against the mirror inside the elevator. "I should've known they'd come after RJ. I should've never left him."

"They had other opportunities to get him, and never made an attempt. They decided to make a move once they figured you'd gotten your hands on the information they wanted. How were you supposed to know that?"

When the elevator doors opened, Gina walked silently to the door of her mother's place and then turned to him, grabbing handfuls of his shirt. "We're going to give it to them, aren't we, Josh?"

"I'm going to get RJ back for you. Count on it. They told your mother to meet us at the airport and break the news to you immediately, didn't they?"

"Yeah, that's what she said." She unlocked the door, and they entered the empty condo.

"They wanted to make sure we knew they had RJ before we turned over the information to the CIA. They don't want to hurt him. They wanted to give you that chance."

"What if they've already hurt him?" She swept up one of RJ's trucks from the floor and collapsed onto the sofa, hugging it to her chest.

"Of course, they're going to have to show some proof that he's okay before we even deal with them." He leaned over the back of the sofa and massaged her shoulders.

"When is that going to be? What are they waiting for?"

"The right time. I know it's hard, but try to be patient."

She spun one of the wheels of the truck. "You're not just going to hand over the plans, are you? They're too important. They're what you came for, why the government sent you here in the first place."

"I'll work something out. RJ's safety is the most important thing right now."

"It's the only thing to me."

"I know that." He twisted his head around. "Where's your phone? Keep an eye on it since you could be contacted at any time."

She patted the pocket of the sweater she'd

hugged around her body since they'd returned, like she was trying to warm up. "Right here. Believe me, I'm not going anywhere without it."

"I suppose it won't do much good for you to get information about Diego's family from the daycare. It'll all be lies anyway, and we don't want to alert his kidnappers that we're probing."

"Josh." She placed the truck on the floor and wandered to the window, twisting her fingers in front of her. "How would the terrorists know that we gave the info to the CIA? They don't even know what they're looking for. They don't know the weapons are in a tunnel. They don't even know about the tunnel. What if we just turned over the plans to your superiors and pretended to give Los Santos's and Vlad's people vital information that was actually worthless?"

"First, they're not going to release RJ without some solid proof that you know where the drugs and weapons are. Second, don't discount the idea that they're not going to know what the CIA is up to. Computer hacking, leaks, moles—these are all real concerns in the intelligence community. Just as we monitor their chatter, they monitor ours."

"I thought as much." She burrowed back into the sofa. Hunching her shoulders, she buried herself deeper into her sweater.

That was not the answer she'd wanted from

him, but he wasn't going to risk RJ's life…and he wasn't going to let the CIA or Ariel risk that child's life either.

He couldn't watch her sitting comatose in the corner of that sofa just waiting and worrying.

"Let's order something to eat. We haven't had anything since Fernanda fed us lunch, and that seems like a lifetime ago."

"We can't leave. I'm not walking out of here with RJ missing to have a meal."

"I said *order*. Pizza?"

She flicked her fingers. "Whatever you like. I can't stomach the thought of food."

He crossed the room to pick up Joanna's landline, holding up the buzzing receiver. "Any recommendations?"

"Supreme Pizza." She pulled out her cell phone. "The number's in here."

Not wanting to tie up her phone, he punched in the number on the landline and handed Gina's cell back to her. When he gave the pizza place Joanna's phone number, the guy on the phone already knew the address.

"Extra-large pepperoni and a house salad, Italian dressing." He glanced at Gina and she shrugged.

While they waited for the pizza, Josh typed up some notes on his laptop and Gina watched TV without seeing a thing. Josh shot a few worried glances her way. He almost wished she'd wail and gnash her teeth in her grief. It would be easier to comfort her.

Right now she looked as brittle as a dried stalk of wheat that, once touched, would break apart and scatter. If that happened, he'd lose her for sure.

He didn't know what Vlad's people were waiting for, but he was almost certain it *was* Vlad who had RJ and not Los Santos. The drug dealers were much less discreet than the terrorists—and not as highly trained.

The buzzer for the front door of the building startled them both, and Josh shoved away from the counter where he'd been working to press the speaker button. "Yeah?"

"Pizza delivery for Joanna."

"Stay there. I'll be right down."

Gina looked over the pillow she was hugging to her chest. "My mom usually lets him in and invites him up."

"Not this time. I'll be right back."

Josh stuffed some cash in his pocket and dashed downstairs to the lobby, waving at the security guard on duty. He opened the door for the pizza guy just as a couple was coming through the front door.

"Thanks and keep the change." Josh handed the kid some money and put the bag with the salad on top of the big pizza box and carried it to the elevator.

Back in the condo, he dished some salad into bowls and tossed a couple of pieces of pizza onto two plates. "Come and join me at the counter. I'll even throw in a glass of red wine."

"I couldn't…"

"What? Eat or drink while your son is missing?" He pulled out one of the high stools tucked beneath the center island in the kitchen. "C'mon. You'll need your strength when that call comes through, and a little wine will help you relax while we wait."

She tossed her security pillow to the side and shuffled to the counter. "Why haven't they called? Where is he?"

"They'll call. They want that info and they're not going to jeopardize that by harming RJ." He poured a glass half-full of a red wine he'd found on a small wine rack beneath the island counter. "Drink."

She sipped the wine, closing her eyes. Then she took a bigger gulp and set down the glass with a sigh.

"Already unwound a few of those muscles, right?"

Cupping the glass with both hands, she said, "I'm scared."

"I know you are, Gina." He brushed his fingers along her arm. "You'd be crazy not to be worried, but we got this—and then they'll pay. I'll make them pay."

A cell phone buzzed and he and Gina locked eyes for a few seconds.

She plunged her hand in her pocket, bobbling her phone and almost dropping it before holding it in front of her face. "Unknown number."

"It's them. Speaker."

She nodded and swallowed. "Hello?"

"What did you collect from that bank, Gina? And is it worth your son's life?"

Chapter Seventeen

Gina's heart hammered so loudly in her chest she could hardly hear her own response. "I have the information you want. Where's my son?"

"He's fine. Playing with his companion, Diego."

"I need to speak to him. I need to see him."

The man spoke away from the phone. "Isabella, bring the boy here."

A woman's voice cooed in the background. "It's your mama. Say hello."

"Hi, Mama."

Gina's throat closed with tears, which overflowed from her eyes. "RJ, how are you? Are you having fun?"

"Playing with Diego. We ate hamburgers."

"Lucky." She dashed a tear from her cheek with a balled-up fist. "Where are you?"

"At Diego's."

The sound of a clicking tongue came over the

line. "Did you really think RJ was going to give you directions? As you can tell, he's fine. Now, what did you pick up at the bank?"

Josh tapped her phone and then pointed to his eyes.

"I—I want to see RJ."

"For God's sake. The boy is fine." After some noise in the background, the man heaved a heavy sigh. "All right."

A minute later, a picture of RJ holding a French fry and smiling came over the phone, and Gina traced his precious face with her finger.

The man growled, "Well?"

Josh had been writing on napkins and shoved the first one at her.

She read from the napkin. "'The weapons and the drugs are in a tunnel.'"

There was a sharp intake of breath over the phone. "A tunnel, where?"

Josh tapped the paper and she read the words he'd written. "'A tunnel beneath the US–Mexican border.'"

The man cursed in a language other than English, other than Spanish, and Gina gripped the phone tighter. Los Santos didn't have RJ, the terrorists did.

"Where is it? Do you have a map?" He paused for a few seconds. "You didn't already turn this information over to that navy SEAL or the CIA, did you? Because if you did…"

"No!" She knew the end of that sentence and didn't want to hear it, didn't even want to think it. "I mean, my… The SEAL knows because he was there with me. He's here now."

Josh leaned toward the phone. "What should stop us from turning this over to the US government? Why wouldn't we, and just lie to you about it? How would you know one way or the other?"

"Oh, we'd know. That's why this kid is still alive. We haven't heard anything, otherwise."

"You have a mole?"

"Where's the tunnel?"

"Where's Gina's son?"

"She'll get him back, safe and sound, once we get our weapons, the weapons her lying, cheating father stole from us. If the CIA hadn't killed Hector De Santos, we would've done it for them. We'd upheld our end of the deal and delivered the drugs and he didn't turn over the weapons, as planned. You can blame your father for all of this."

Gina covered her eyes with her hand. She blamed them all.

"Listen—" Josh picked up the phone "—you're not getting this information until RJ is in his mother's arms. We'll meet you in Mexico. We'll guide you in from there once Gina has her son."

Lifting her hand, Gina peeked at Josh. He was serious. They were all going to meet out by this tunnel in Mexico.

The man on the other end of the line grunted. "That could work, but if you call in the CIA, the FBI, the DEA, the US military, we'll know about it—and the deal is off and things won't end well for Hector De Santos's grandson."

Gina put her hands to her ears and suppressed a moan that had started deep in her gut.

Josh stroked her hair. "I believe you. We won't call anyone."

Josh spent the rest of the conversation telling the man, who called himself Yuri, where to meet them in the Sonoran Desert and working out a plan for an exchange.

When Josh ended the call, Gina folded her arms across her stomach. "What are you going to do? You're not going to allow a band of terrorists to walk away with a cache of weapons, are you?"

"No. I don't think Los Santos is going to allow it either."

"What do you mean?"

"I told the scumbag on the phone that I wouldn't tell any government agency and I won't, but I don't think the terrorists have a mole within Los Santos. Do you?"

"You're going to tell Los Santos to meet us there, too?" She put one hand to her throat where her pulse was beating wildly. "That could put RJ in so much danger."

"RJ's already in danger. We have to have some element of surprise on our side."

"Why would Los Santos trust you? They can't possibly believe you're going to allow them to keep the drugs once they take out Vlad's people—*if* they can take out Vlad's people."

"Maybe we broker our own kind of deal with Los Santos. Vlad knows who I am, but the drug dealers don't. They don't know you're working with anyone. You can play them off."

"Me?" She jabbed an index finger at her chest just to make sure. "How can I play them off? What does that even mean?"

"As far as they know, you're Hector De Santos's daughter and Ricky Rojas's widow. You were more than eager to meet up with them when you thought Ricky might still be alive. I'm the jealous boyfriend who wouldn't allow it."

"You want me to contact the cartel, don't you? You want me to make some kind of deal with them."

"You can turn to them. Tell them the terrorist group has kidnapped your son, Hector De

Santos's grandson and the heir apparent to Los Santos. You want your son back, you want revenge and you want those drugs."

She had to take another swig of wine for this one. "What about you?"

"Like I said, they don't know who I am. Why wouldn't you seek the protection of Los Santos? The last remaining members heard of you, you were at your father's compound in Colombia when he and your husband were shot and killed. You were grilled by the DEA and never gave up anyone or anything."

"That's because I didn't know anything."

"They don't know that. Besides, you knew about the accounts on Isla Perdida and kept mum about those."

"How are we going to pull this off without endangering RJ?"

"We'll keep RJ safe. We'll have to arrange some kind of ambush by Los Santos after you have possession of RJ."

"Los Santos will get away with the drugs. You know that, don't you? How could you live with yourself if you allowed that to happen, after all you've been through, after what your family went through at the hands of my father's cartel?"

"The DEA can always go after the cartel. Stopping Vlad is more important right now. Los

Santos is the lesser of two evils. We know the location of the tunnel, and the DEA can come in and shut it down.

"It'll work." He popped a pizza crust in his mouth. "We'll make it work."

"Will it satisfy the people you report to?"

"It will hinder Vlad, and that's what they care about."

"Los Santos will want those weapons back."

"They're not going to get them. That I can't allow."

"You have a plan for those, I suppose?"

"Oh, yeah. Think about it." He crumpled a napkin and fired it into the lid of the pizza box. "We have a huge advantage over both Vlad and Los Santos—we're the only ones who know the location of that tunnel."

"What do we do next?"

"Before we fly out to Tucson tomorrow, you're going to contact Los Santos. Reply to the number they used to text you. Tell them you need their help and are willing to turn over Hector's drugs to get it."

"I hope they believe me."

"Why wouldn't they? You were afraid of them before. You thought they were going to kill you for information you didn't have—now you do have it."

"The people in Isla Perdida—were they Vlad's or the cartel's?"

"I think the man in the red tie who conveniently passed out on the plane was Los Santos. The couple and the assassin in the boat were Vlad."

"And you?"

"I'm just the jealous boyfriend who wants a little piece of the action."

Licking the taste of spicy pepperoni from her lips, Gina eyed her cell phone. "Should I do it now?"

"Send them a text."

They worked out the text together on the napkin first, and then Gina entered it into her phone.

I know where the drugs are. They have RJ. I need help.

She held her breath as the message zipped through. If this didn't work, she could die. RJ could die. She had to trust that Josh wouldn't let that happen. She had to trust the man who had killed RJ's father.

Gina stared at the display on her phone until her eyes grew tired and dry, until Josh had cleaned up all the dishes and wrapped up the pizza, until her wineglass was full again.

"Go to bed." Josh brushed a finger across her lips. "They're not going to answer any faster with you staring at the phone."

She dragged her gaze away from the cell. "What if Los Santos doesn't answer at all? What if they don't believe me?"

"They want those drugs. That haul represents millions and millions of dollars to them and their street cred. If Los Santos wants to ride again, they need to prove they have the goods and the guts to carry on without the brains behind the operation."

"I hope you're right, or we'll be going out to Mexico tomorrow to face Vlad's people with nothing." She cupped her phone in her hand just as it buzzed, and she jumped.

Josh raised his brows at her, but she shook her head. "It's a text from Mom. Should I tell her I talked to RJ?"

"Don't tell her anything."

She responded to her mother and then dumped the rest of her wine in the sink. She needed a clear head to confront what was coming her way.

As they both turned to face the stairs, she grabbed Josh's hand. "Stay the night with me? I can't be alone."

"You're not alone." He placed his hands on her hips and followed her up the stairs.

Later in bed, she nestled her back against

Josh, whose arm was draped around her waist. "I wonder if RJ is afraid. I wonder if he knows something isn't right."

"His captors are going to do everything in their power to make him comfortable. They have to bring him to Mexico, and they don't want an uncooperative subject. I'm sure they're telling him he's going to meet you there. He's probably still with Diego."

"Whoever that child is." Gina squeezed her eyes shut, trying to block out the guilt she felt for sending RJ into the unknown.

Just as she started to drift off, Josh's arm still securely around her, the cell phone in her hand buzzed.

She jerked awake and Josh said, "Is it them?"

Peering at the screen glowing in the dark, she read aloud from the text. "'Welcome home, *paloma*.'"

THE NEXT DAY, Gina stood in the middle of the Sonoran Desert as the wind whipped her hair across her face and sand pelted the back of her neck.

While they were in Arizona, Josh had called upon a buddy of his, a retired marine who'd worked bomb demolition. Josh had explained that Connor Delancey not only knew how to take apart explosives, he knew how to put them together.

Gina squinted through the binoculars at the rocks guarding the cave's entrance and said a little prayer for Josh and Connor as they rigged explosives among the weapons and drugs that were tucked inside the miles-long tunnel beneath the earth. Without her father's map, the location would be completely hidden.

She hoped RJ was miles away from that tunnel when it blew. They were counting on Los Santos to provide a diversion and some chaos so that Josh could get away from the tunnel and trigger the explosion.

Movement near the entrance of the tunnel had her tightening the grip on her .22. When Josh waved his arms over his head, she sagged with relief even though they still had a long way to go.

Five minutes later, the two men were back in Connor's four-wheel drive.

"Did everything go okay? Do you think it's going to work?"

"As long as this guy does his job as well as I've done mine." Connor jabbed Josh in the ribs with the end of a stick he'd picked up on his way into the tunnel.

Gina grabbed her hair with one hand, holding it in a ponytail. "How long?"

Josh checked his watch. "Two hours before I give Vlad's people their final directions to this spot in the desert."

Connor clapped Josh on the back. "Do me a favor, dude."

"Let me guess—pictures?"

"You got that right." Connor framed his hands in the air. "Just the moment it all detonates."

"Hopefully, we're going to be too far away to get any good pictures."

"C'mon, man. You're going to deny an artist his moment in the sun."

"You've got issues, Connor. I'll do what I can."

Josh shook Connor's hand, and Connor pulled him in for a one-armed, manly hug. "Hope it works out for you. If you need anything else on the other side of the border, let me know. And remember—" he winked at Gina "—I was never here."

Gina threw her arms around the big man. "Thank you so much. We couldn't have done this without you."

He took her by the shoulders. "I'd do anything for Josh Elliott. The man saved so many lives, including my own. Take a life, save a life."

She nodded, tears pricking the backs of her eyes. That's exactly what Josh had done for her.

Several minutes later, Josh took her hand as

they stood side by side watching the dust from Connor's four-wheel drive disperse across the desert sand.

"It's just us now." She pressed the side of her head against his arm.

"Us and—" he walked to their Jeep and lifted a huge case from the back "—this. I'm going to set up now."

"Should I go with you?"

He pointed to some rock outcroppings in the distance. "We're going right there. Your father couldn't have picked a better place for his tunnel."

"That's driving distance, especially in this terrain."

"That's the point. Nobody can see or figure out what we're doing from that distance." He leveled a finger at the rocks.

"What if…?"

He held up a hand. "We'll work through anything that comes up."

She swung into the Jeep beside him and they bounced over the uneven ground, heading for a pile of rocks that resembled the discarded building blocks of some playful giants.

Josh parked the Jeep at the base of the outcropping and hauled his sniper rifle from the back. She followed him up and over the granite until he reached a flattop.

"Are you going to be able to get here in time?"

Josh ignored her question, and Gina perched on a rock, watching him pull pieces of his weapon out of the case and set it up on the flat base of the rock. Had he gone through the same motions on a hillside outside her father's compound in Colombia?

His eye to the scope, he tweaked and shifted the rifle several times before letting out a long breath. "Got it."

"What if there's someone standing in the way? What if they notice the trigger wire at the tunnel's entrance and yank it out?"

"I doubt anyone's going to be yanking any wires, even if they see them. They'll take off running before they do that. And I'll make sure nobody is standing in the way."

"You do this sort of thing all the time? Set up these types of ambushes?"

"I'm an old pro."

"How much time?"

"Just enough time to get you up here and show you what to do."

Gina froze. "What are you talking about?"

"I'm going to train you to be a sniper in fifteen minutes."

She blinked. She stood up. She plopped back down on the rock. "You're not serious."

"I'm deadly serious." He held out his hand to

her. "Do you really think Vlad's people or Los Santos for that matter, are going to allow me to leave that tunnel?"

"Th-they're not going to kill you."

"Vlad would like nothing better than to kill me." He cupped his fingers and gestured her forward. "You have to do this, Gina. It's all set up for you. I've done the hard part. All you have to do is pull the trigger."

"You're crazy." She shook her head back and forth, hoping to clear it.

"I'm not gonna lie. The kickback on the rifle's gonna be a bitch, but you're a strong woman and you can handle it. If it knocks you on your ass after you take the shot, that's okay. You just need the one shot, and then you take RJ and get the hell out of here."

"You mean, after I pick you up."

"Yeah, yeah. After you pick me up."

"Josh…"

He took her hand. "C'mon up and let me show you what to do."

Gina spent the next several minutes with her eye to the scope, her finger on the trigger of the big rifle and a knot in her stomach. Josh actually expected her to shoot the sniper rifle at the trigger he and Connor had propped up between two rocks, setting off an explosion in the tunnel.

And then he expected her to, what? Leave

him behind? Knowing his life could be in her hands gave her more courage and determination than she'd ever had before in her life.

After he had her run through the instructions with him for about the hundredth time, she collapsed on a rock and stretched out her fingers.

"I think you've got it down. You can do this." He sat beside her and rested his hand on her thigh.

She glanced down at his hand and trailed her fingers along the corded muscle of his forearm. She wasn't ready to lose Josh yet. There was too much she had to tell him.

The pressure of her touch increased as a sudden panic rushed through her body.

Josh's head shifted slightly to the side as he raised his eyebrows. "You okay?"

"Whatever happens today, just know that I love you, Josh Elliott."

He grabbed her face with both hands and pulled her close. "God, and I thought it was just me who'd fallen in love with you."

Chapter Eighteen

Josh's muscles tensed as he spied the headlights in the distance. Nighttime hadn't fallen in the desert yet, but any minute now it would come on fast like a curtain dropping on a stage.

Gina sat up in the passenger seat of the Jeep. "Is that them?"

"Can't imagine who else it would be out here," Josh mouthed the words around the toothpick in the side of his mouth, and then spit it out. "Are you ready?"

"I'm ready to see RJ."

Tugging on her hair, he pulled her close and kissed her hard on the mouth. "This is gonna work."

"I know. I believe that with all my heart."

"Then it's showtime." He launched out of the Jeep onto the desert floor and called back to Gina. "Two vehicles."

She exited the car and stood beside him,

crossing her arms. "One of those cars better have RJ in it."

"They passed the rocks where the rifle is stationed." He rolled his shoulders. One victory at a time.

The two off-road vehicles came in hot, kicking up a dust storm in their wake. The first truck carried a man, standing and pointing a rifle at them.

The knots in Josh's gut tightened as he spread his arms out to his sides. He'd already disarmed himself, his weapons, except for the sniper rifle hidden in the rocks, displayed on the hood of the Jeep.

A bright white light mounted on the first truck bathed the area in an eerie glow. The vehicles squealed to a stop, and Josh huffed out a breath when he saw a woman lead RJ from the second vehicle.

Gina cried out and rushed toward her son, but the man with the rifle waved her off.

"When we say you can."

Gina stopped, her arms stretched out before her. "RJ, are you okay?"

The boy nodded, his eyes wide and glassy. Fun time with Diego must've ended and confusion had set in.

Josh curled his fists at his sides. This had to work.

A man stepped forward and Josh recognized his voice from the phone call. Yuri. "Where is the tunnel? How do we get to it?"

"Release the boy to his mother now, let them both leave as planned and I'll take you over. It's not gonna happen before that and you'll never find the entrance to that tunnel without me."

The ringleader nodded to one of his minions, and he grabbed Josh and patted him down. Then the man took the gun and the knife on top of the Jeep and pocketed them. "You won't be needing these."

The woman, who had to be the one who called herself Rita, said something to RJ and relinquished her grip on his shoulders.

RJ took off like a shot and barreled into his mother's waiting arms.

She stroked RJ's hair and whispered to him.

"Take the Jeep, Gina, and get out of here."

She raised her head and met his gaze. Her eyes were dark pools in her face, but he knew she could do it.

Yuri motioned with his gun. "The tunnel?"

"This way." Josh didn't give Gina another look as she piled RJ into the Jeep beside her and made a U-turn, kicking up sand with her wheels.

He didn't want any of this bunch to realize what Gina meant to him. Hell, he hadn't realized how much she meant to him until she told him she loved him.

Josh wiped a drop of sweat from his brow and picked up his flashlight. "This way, about a quarter of a mile."

He scuffed through the sand toward the tunnel Hector De Santos had constructed for the purpose of allowing terrorists and weapons to enter the United States.

Vlad would never give up something this valuable, so Josh put a little insurance into place to at least give himself a fighting chance to get out of here alive…in case Los Santos didn't follow through.

As he approached the entrance, obscured by the two boulders, Josh turned suddenly to the three men following him. "If Vlad thinks he's going to have use of this tunnel after you remove these weapons, you can set him straight."

Yuri narrowed his eyes. "What do you mean?"

"Before you got here, I videotaped the location of the tunnel on my phone and sent it to my email address. I have an email message set to send automatically in two days, and if I'm not alive and well to stop that message, it will go out to a friend of mine with instructions. You can imagine what those instructions are."

"What's to stop you from sending out that message anyway when…if we let you go?"

"Nothing except my word and your word that Gina De Santos and her son will be safe as long as you get what you want here tonight."

"We intend to get what we want, and Vlad will get what he wants."

The corner of Josh's eye twitched. What Vlad wanted was to kill one of the navy SEALs from the team that had dogged him all over the Middle East.

Josh continued to the two innocuous-looking rocks and aimed his flashlight at the entrance, careful to keep the light away from the two rocks that held the trigger box.

"I see it, Yuri. I see how to get into the tunnel." One of Yuri's henchmen pushed Josh to the side where he stumbled against the two rocks. Perfect—now he could stand in front of the trigger mechanism, blocking it from view.

Yuri stood back as the man shoved aside one of the boulders, already leveraged to move with ease.

"Watch him." Yuri ducked inside the tunnel and one of the men followed him, while the other stayed at the entrance with Josh.

Out of the corner of his eye, Josh detected movement by the vehicles. Rita and one other had stayed behind with the cars, but they would be no match for the members of the cartel, intent on getting their drugs.

The man holding Josh at gunpoint hadn't noticed the commotion yet, didn't know what to look for in the rapidly darkening desert.

The tunnel interested the guy much more. He cupped a hand around his mouth and yelled, "Are they there? Are the weapons there?"

Yuri called back, "Everything De Santos promised and even all the drugs we gave him... and I'm guessing this tunnel leads straight into Arizona."

Finally the man guarding him noticed the three figures slipping toward them in the shadows.

"What the hell?" Those were the last words out of his mouth—forever. He dropped in front of Josh, and Josh leaped over the rocks housing the trigger box and started crawling through the sand.

"Hey, hey!"

Someone else shouted in Spanish and a gunshot rang out.

Josh was not waiting around to see who was shooting at what. At some point they'd reach a standoff, and both parties probably figured they'd be able to catch up with him and kill him out here in the desert.

But they weren't figuring on Gina De Santos.

PANTING, GINA REACHED the lookout. She'd left RJ snug in the back seat of the Jeep, wrapped in a blanket.

She put her eye to the scope of the sniper rifle, and it framed exactly what it was supposed to frame. She had to stop herself from moving it to look for Josh to make sure he was out of the way.

He'd assured her he'd be long gone, but he would've told her that anyway. He was only half expecting to make it out of this desert alive. He was willing to sacrifice himself to destroy the weapons and the drugs, to destroy that tunnel… and to protect her and RJ.

She licked her lips. She planned to get Josh out of here in one piece and it started with one shot.

With her eye pressed to the scope, just as Josh had taught her, she curled her finger around the trigger. The night vision on the scope made everything at the tunnel as clear as day, and she saw two men disappear into what looked like the solid face of a rock. Another man had a gun pointed at Josh. She couldn't look at that.

All her focus, and the rifle's, was on the box wedged between two rocks at Josh's feet. He'd instructed her to shoot when she saw Los Santos on the scene, regardless of where he was or what he was doing.

Fat chance.

The man holding Josh at gunpoint dropped. Two flashes of light flared near the tunnel entrance. She could no longer see Josh's feet near the two rocks. Did that mean he'd gotten away? Followed the men into the tunnel? Gotten himself shot?

Josh's voice growled in her ear. *Don't think. Take the shot.*

With a sob she braced her feet against a boulder behind her and pulled the trigger of the sniper rifle.

The kickback on the rifle almost ripped her arm from its socket and she stumbled backward, the boulder catching her fall. She made a hard landing on the rock just as the night sky exploded with a red-and-orange cloud.

Staggering to her feet, she gaped at the flames and smoke cascading up to the desert sky.

"Mama!"

Leaving the rifle, she scampered down the rocks to the Jeep and vaulted into the driver's seat. "Are you okay, RJ?"

"Look. Fireworks."

"You're right. Someone set off some fireworks, all right."

She mumbled a few prayers as she cranked on the Jeep's engine. Josh had told her to wait here for him after the explosion, and he'd make his way back.

Not one chance in hell.

She flicked on the high beams and followed the well-worn trail back toward the original meeting place, a gun on the passenger seat beside her. If Los Santos hadn't taken out Rita and whoever else stayed behind, Gina would be ready for them.

And if any of Vlad's men had Josh in their clutches, she'd be ready for them, too.

Her lights picked out a figure running, the orange glow behind him, the sand dragging down his every step. Holding her breath, Gina slowed down and grabbed the gun.

"Are we going to the fireworks, Mama?"

"Maybe we are, little frog."

The figure waved his arms and Gina let out a sob as she recognized Josh's handsome face with the biggest smile she'd ever seen plastered on it. She made a U-turn and then pulled up alongside him.

He'd stopped, bending over with his hands on his knees, gulping in air.

She leaned over and opened the passenger door. "Goin' my way, SEAL?"

Epilogue

Gina stretched her arms toward the sun and then adjusted her red bikini top. Cupping one hand over her eyes, she yelled toward the pool, "Not so close to the edge."

Josh, with RJ on his shoulders, turned and then both of them splashed water at her at the same time.

"You two!" She laughed and tipped up her sunglasses. "RJ, come and eat your lunch."

"C'mon, big guy." Josh swam to the edge of the pool, towing RJ behind him. "Time to eat lunch. We can go out again, unless you want to visit the turtles on the beach first."

"Turtles, turtles!"

"You got it." Josh lifted RJ out of the pool and placed him on the deck.

Gina patted the chaise longue to her left. "Come and dry off."

RJ clambered into the chaise longue, pulling

a towel around his wet body, and a minute later the poolside waitress delivered lunch.

Gina made sure RJ had everything he needed and then took a sip of her tequila sunrise. She held up the glass to Josh toweling off his hair on the other side of her. "Kind of decadent to have a froufrou drink in the middle of the afternoon."

"We're on vacation, and you deserve it."

Once Josh's superiors had received his report and were satisfied that the weapons Hector De Santos was once going to deliver to Vlad's terrorist organization had been destroyed, along with the drugs he'd gotten in exchange for those weapons, they sent Josh on a short leave before he had to return to his deployment overseas.

They'd decided to join Gina's mother and Tom in the Bahamas, and RJ couldn't have been happier with the arrangement. For having no father as a role model, Josh had picked up the part quickly.

Josh clinked his beer mug against her glass. "Don't get too comfortable behind that sniper rifle. My commanding officer just might send you out in the field."

"Where you're going." She smoothed a hand down his shoulder. "I'm going to worry about you."

"That's the hard part—for you. It's almost easier being out there than sitting at home waiting." He kissed the inside of her wrist. "I hear that all the time from the guys who have partners. Their wives and girlfriends are the ones who do all the hard work."

"I don't want you to be thinking about that, about me. I'm going to have plenty to keep me busy, finding a spot for my new bar now that the DEA released my grandmother's money to me."

"Impossible for me to not think about you, but I'll be imagining you starting your new venture and not worrying about me. Deal?"

"Works for me. Everything about you works for me, Josh."

"Was Joanna upset you turned the accounts in Isla Perdida over to the DEA?"

"No—resigned. When I told some of what we went through and what Hector had been planning, she didn't want the money anymore. Besides, Tom has enough for the both of them. What about Vlad?"

His jaw tightened. "What about him?"

"Did all this bring the CIA...or Ariel any closer to finding him?"

"No. He has his minions do the dirty work. He pulls the strings behind the scenes. But more and more, he's making his presence known and he's going to slip up. When he does—" Josh snapped his fingers "—we'll be there."

"With so many people on his trail, it's bound

to happen. Was the CIA able to bring in any of the people who followed us to the island?"

"They picked up Roger and Tara—surprisingly not their real names. The man in the red tie?" He shrugged. "Melted away."

"But they did get Rita. Poor Diego. His own mother used him to get to RJ."

"Diego is safe with his grandmother now."

Gina shivered. "RJ could've wound up like Diego if my father and Ricky had lived."

"But they didn't." Josh raised his glass and took a sip of his drink. "Let's try to enjoy these few days we have together. Joanna promised that she and Tom would stay with RJ tonight while I take you out for some dinner, dancing and a moonlit stroll along the beach—and RJ's staying in their room."

"I can't wait." She'd enjoy every second with Josh until he had to leave her, and then she'd send him off with love and the belief that he'd do his job to the best of his ability and come home to her.

Josh held up the sunscreen. "Can you get my back?"

She winked. "I'll always have your back, SEAL."

And she knew he'd always have hers.

* * * * *

Look for the next book in Carol Ericson's
RED, WHITE AND BUILT *miniseries,*
POINT BLANK SEAL, *on sale next month!*

*And don't miss the first two books
in the miniseries:*

LOCKED, LOADED AND SEALED
ALPHA BRAVO SEAL

*You'll find them wherever
Harlequin Intrigue books are sold!*

Get 2 Free Books,
Plus 2 Free Gifts—

just for trying the Reader Service!

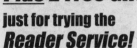

Get 2 Free Books,
Plus 2 Free Gifts—
just for trying the Reader Service!

HARLEQUIN *Romance*

YES! Please send me 2 FREE Harlequin® Romance LARGER PRINT novels and my 2 FREE gifts (gifts are worth about $10 retail). After receiving them, if I don't wish to receive any more books, I can return the shipping statement marked "cancel." If I don't cancel, I will receive 4 brand-new novels every month and be billed just $5.34 per book in the U.S. or $5.74 per book in Canada. That's a savings of at least 15% off the cover price! It's quite a bargain! Shipping and handling is just 50¢ per book in the U.S. and 75¢ per book in Canada.* I understand that accepting the 2 free books and gifts places me under no obligation to buy anything. I can always return a shipment and cancel at any time. The free books and gifts are mine to keep no matter what I decide.

119/319 HDN GLWP

Name _____ (PLEASE PRINT)

Address _____ Apt. #

City _____ State/Prov. _____ Zip/Postal Code

Signature (if under 18, a parent or guardian must sign)

Mail to the **Reader Service:**

IN U.S.A.: P.O. Box 1341, Buffalo, NY 14240-8531
IN CANADA: P.O. Box 603, Fort Erie, Ontario L2A 5X3

**Want to try two free books from another line?
Call 1-800-873-8635 or visit www.ReaderService.com.**

* Terms and prices subject to change without notice. Prices do not include applicable taxes. Sales tax applicable in N.Y. Canadian residents will be charged applicable taxes. Offer not valid in Quebec. This offer is limited to one order per household. Books received may not be as shown. Not valid for current subscribers to Harlequin Romance Larger-Print books. All orders subject to approval. Credit or debit balances in a customer's account(s) may be offset by any other outstanding balance owed by or to the customer. Please allow 4 to 6 weeks for delivery. Offer available while quantities last.

Your Privacy—The Reader Service is committed to protecting your privacy. Our Privacy Policy is available online at www.ReaderService.com or upon request from the Reader Service.

We make a portion of our mailing list available to reputable third parties that offer products we believe may interest you. If you prefer that we not exchange your name with third parties, or if you wish to clarify or modify your communication preferences, please visit us at www.ReaderService.com/consumerschoice or write to us at Reader Service Preference Service, P.O. Box 9062, Buffalo, NY 14240-9062. Include your complete name and address.

HRLP17R2

Get 2 Free Books,

MYSTERY WORLDWIDE LIBRARY®

Plus 2 Free Gifts—

just for trying the Reader Service!

WWLI7R